PRAISE FOR *VORACIOUS*

"*Voracious* is phenomenal. I am blown away. Like totally blown away. Belicia Rhea is insanely gifted, a phenomenal creative force, a rare talent. This is absolutely unforgettable, off the charts. Wow!"

—Caroline Kepnes, *New York Times* bestselling author of *You*

"Belicia Rhea paints startling and masterful visions of trauma and secrets. Her debut novella is a triumph of storytelling, committed to both heart-achingly sympathetic characters and its obsessive pursuit of crescendoing horror. *Voracious* is as sharp as the sting of a wasp, and make no mistake, it will paralyze you with its venom. Never has blight and entomophobia read so gorgeously on the page."

—Christa Carmen, two-time Bram Stoker-nominated author of *The Daughters of Block Island*

"*Voracious* is a claustrophobic exploration of bodily autonomy, of the body as a prison. Rhea peels back the darkest corners of the mind, revealing unseen scars. The novella pries at human irrationality, compulsion, and vulnerability, illuminating how the claws of paranoia sew, stitch each of our fears into our skin so we may never forget them."

—Ai Jiang, Nebula, Bram Stoker, BSFA, and Locus Award finalist, and author of *Linghun* and *I AM AI*

"Belicia Rhea's *Voracious* is a beautifully layered study of surrender to rising insanity, altered reality, and apocalyptic invasion. This is Weird fiction at its finest. Highly recommended."

—Nancy Holder, winner of the Horror Writers Association Lifetime Achievement Award

"*Voracious* is a compact knot of phobias and trauma. Rhea grips the reader by the chin and forces them to confront horrors real and imagined. A compulsively readable nightmare."

—L. P. Hernandez, author of *Stargazers*

"Claustrophobic, gritty and terrifying—with *Voracious*, Belicia Rhea has crafted a compelling and stomach-turning tale of psychological horror. A kickass blend of body horror, madness and apocalyptic dread. I finished it in one sitting."

—Laurel Hightower, author of *Below* and *Crossroads*

"Absolutely mesmerizing. Unputdownable and visceral, *Voracious* dug straight in and broke me open in ways I never saw coming. I loved this book."

—Steph Nelson, author of *The Vein* and *The Final Scene*

"If you weren't scared of bugs before, you will be after reading *Voracious*. Belicia Rhea expertly crafts an intense and disturbing tale of trauma, vulnerability, and paranoia as we follow a pregnant teenage girl tormented by visions of an insect ridden apocalypse. This novella will stick with you, laying eggs of fear that will hatch and skitter free at the sight of every fly, every moth, every screaming cicada."

—Angela Sylvaine, author of *Frost Bite* and
The Dead Spot: Stories of Lost Girls

"Belicia Rhea's harrowing debut novella steadily burrows into the complex interiority of women's lives and surfaces with profound insight into mental illness, trauma, and the way we live today. Like all the most powerful body horror, *Voracious* gets deep under your skin."

—Robert Levy, author of *The Glittering World* and
No One Dies from Love

"Not for the faint of stomach, *Voracious* is a visceral descent into the hell of being female, where the modern meets the ancient."

—Izzy Lee, writer/director of *House of Ashes* and
author of *I Can See Your Lies*

"Gruesome, compassionate, and unflinchingly feminist, Belicia Rhea's debut novella puts her firmly in the ranks of Sara Tantlinger and Hailey Piper while delivering its own vicious brood of nightmares. I read it in one sitting, as disturbed as I was rapt by this unique vision of someone's apocalypse."

—Jaq Evans, author of *What Grows in the Dark*

"Mesmerizing and darkly prophetic, *Voracious* is an apocalyptic nightmare. This novella is a horrifying and ominous depiction of grief, fear, family, and trauma. Insidious, creeping, and sure to ignite paranoia in readers, it begs to be read all in one bite."

—Delaney S. Saul, Associate Editor of
Voyage YA by Uncharted

VORACIOUS

CONTENT WARNINGS

Eating Disorders, Sex, Violence, Abuse, Sexual Abuse, Profanity, Bullying, Death

Reader discretion is advised.

Edited by Rob Carroll
Book Design and Layout by Rob Carroll
Cover Design by Rob Carroll

ISBN 978-1-958598-25-2 (paperback)
ISBN 978-1-958598-71-9 (eBook)

darkmatter-ink.com

VORACIOUS

BELICIA RHEA

CONTENTS

"In a theater, it happened that a fire started off-stage. The clown came out to tell the audience. They thought it was a joke and applauded. He told them again, and they became still more hilarious. This is the way, I suppose, that the world will be destroyed—amid the universal hilarity of wits and wags who think it is all a joke."

—Søren Kierkegaard, *Either/Or: A Fragment of Life*

I

LILA CLAPPED HER hands to her ears and turned from the window so that she was no longer directly in front of it, but not quite facing away. She had to make sure they weren't getting closer. The cicadas blared outside, and she shuddered as if she could feel them crawling along her skin. After waking in a fit from the nightmare vision, she was too rattled to sleep. She'd be exhausted at school, but she figured it didn't really matter. Nothing mattered anymore, with what was coming.

Even if she wanted to risk sleeping, the cicadas were too loud. She hated how their crepitation went on and on, the way they took up so little space and so much all at once. Trying to block out the noise, she flipped a page in the book on her lap and forced herself to concentrate on her research. Reading was an important part of her survival. The more she knew, the more she could prepare.

Lila immersed herself in every book she could find about arachnids, beetles, arthropods, all of them. A book titled *Radioactive Waste: The Colossal Growth of Indestructible Cockroaches* lay mercilessly dog-eared on her bed, with bookmarks squashed between various spine-cracked texts: *The Rise of Insect Colonies, The Crawling Aftermath of Hiroshima and Nagasaki,* sticky notes marked to indistinguishable scribbles all over The King James Version of The Holy Bible. The scrawled cursive of Lila's frantic handwriting read phrases like "the locusts"—"the plagues"—"the return." The stack of books Marcus gave her lay untouched by the baseboard, but she hadn't looked at them in a while, and wasn't sure she wanted to. His notes littered the margins, along with phrases he'd underlined that sometimes made no sense and she couldn't follow, figuring he'd lost his train of thought.

Sitting on her cluttered bed, a sea of pages, she fumbled through the mess and bunched up two pillows behind her back. The blankets were littered with notebooks and pens sinking into the fabric, and she balanced a textbook on the swell of her pregnant belly as she copied a paragraph into her notebook. Her eyes wandered, trying to decipher a note Marcus had scribbled at the bottom of the page.

Like always, her thoughts drifted to him.

During their first encounter on their old elementary school playground, Marcus had forced her to watch him burn ants. Despite this cruelty, she found herself instantly drawn to him, the way he carried himself with a fearlessness she wished she possessed. He'd held the magnifying glass in the blistering 112-degree heat, roasting them and laughing.

"You shouldn't do that," Lila told him as she paced around, the gravel rocks crunching beneath her feet, her hand held over her face trying to shield her eyes from both the searing glare of the sun and the disgusting sight before her. She had been cautiously avoiding the anthills and ant formations, the lines of them marching endlessly to their underground tunnels. Even then, she knew something terrible was going to happen soon. That it wouldn't be long before they'd pour from every crack in the earth, make the green grass look black.

"It will only upset them more," Lila said, growing irritable with the heat of the sun beating down on her skin.

"Please don't! Why are you still doing it?" she tried pleading with him, this mean boy who couldn't be bothered to even acknowledge her.

"Because," he finally said as he wiped sweat from his brow. "It's them or us."

She could never shake that cavalier look on his face. It haunted her, but not worse than the visions of the swarms, or the thought of masses of them multiplying each passing moment. She knew Marcus was right, deep down. So, she attached herself to Marcus, and clung to him for another ten years. When the droves came in the summers, he would send them away.

Even when she couldn't see them, she knew where they were. Crawling inside the dry wall, making their way into her mouth unexpectedly, living on her eyelashes, hiding in the carpet underneath her bed, creeping through cracks in the ceiling and floors. She'd often seen them in the kitchen cabinets, especially those little mealworms that settled into older bags of flour. Lila didn't eat anything her mother made with flour for this reason. She wouldn't eat many foods for this reason. At least, not without throwing it up after. When she wasn't sticking her fingers down her throat, the morning sickness purged the contents in her stomach for her.

Frustrated that she couldn't focus, she was suddenly dizzy with starvation. She'd been fighting a binge all night, her books failing to distract her.

Normally, Lila's binge-and-purge episodes took place well into the dead of night, but it was almost too late now. She'd have to make it work with only an hour and a half until her mother woke up. Glancing down the hall to confirm Vivian was asleep, she rushed to the kitchen and stacked six slices of leftover pizza onto a plate. Setting it in the microwave, she waited for the numbers on the screen to dwindle, impatiently opening the door even though it still had thirty seconds left to heat.

She barely took two steps into her bedroom before shoveling the slices into her mouth, trying to satiate the emptiness inside of her, the never-ending buzzing. The cheese was barely melted, the pizza cold in spots. She felt protest from her growing belly, but she couldn't stop.

After inhaling the pizza and locking herself in the bathroom, Lila prepared to purge. Waiting for the food to settle, she examined her body in the mirror, the mark on her thigh, her enormous belly she felt a true hatred for. Tying up her hair, she knelt at the toilet, face perched over the lid, elbows bruising from pressing her weight down, her hand brought to her mouth. The action almost appeared prayer-like, both in intention and posture. Complete with a silent reverence, and the overwhelming guilt. *What was I thinking eating a greasy pizza? How many weevils and flies and god knows what else could be infesting that pizza place?*

After the first round of vomiting, she felt a little lighter. Her eyes watered from the sinus irritation, and she had to stop to blow her nose. After rinsing the tomato sauce puke off her hand in the sink, she gave one more jab down her throat. This time, it was like breaking a seal, and a river wanted to come up. Still, some of it was resisting, sitting in her esophagus. Without even removing her fingers, she held them there, relying on her disgust with herself, and finally, more came up after a few seconds of strained retching.

She took her fingers out of her mouth so she could breathe. This time she didn't bother to rinse off her hand,

A reddish slime coated the outside of it, slick with saliva stringing between her fingers. There wasn't normally blood in her vomit, only when she purged too carelessly, but since the pizza had been slathered in tomato sauce, even if it was blood, it was impossible to tell. Usually, the iron taste of blood was somewhat distinguishable, but she'd been throwing up so much lately and a lot of bile started coming up and her nose was running smears of thin snot down her Cupid's bow and the pizza taste overpowered everything into some oblivion of puke-blood-pizza-slop, so to feel better about this, she assumed this was only tomato sauce, definitely not any bleeding or micro tearing of her esophageal lining.

Once more, she slid her vomit-slicked fingers down her throat, determined to get it all up. Sometimes it wasn't bad, like getting to eat a second time, to taste the food again. She wavered between repulsion and thrill of getting to have this post-food, how minutes ago it was still in solid form, that this wasn't so different.

Taking a break, her heart palpitations fluttered and she drank a few gulps of water, her throat swollen. She would have to sit in the shower to finish the rest of this, because she felt weak, like she couldn't hold herself up anymore.

She pulled back the shower curtain and turned the knob of the showerhead on. She stood under the stream of water, belly hiding her feet and forcing her to lean forward to avoid getting vomit all over herself, another obstacle of her size. Of her condition. She couldn't even throw up in peace anymore. Usually, she'd take baths if she wanted to force herself to avoid purging, because even at her lowest, she wasn't going to bathe in her own puke water. That way, she couldn't look directly at the drain, and it couldn't tempt her. *It's okay,* it beckoned. *You can throw up. No one will know. No one can hear you over the sloshing water. It'll all go down the drain. Just like your life. Like the bugs. It'll disappear to where they all live. In the dark, wet places. You need to feed them. Tell them to stay down there. To never come out.*

For a moment, she closed her eyes, the water pattering against her face. When she opened them, she eyed the drain and stuck two fingers down her throat, pressing hard against the flap covering her windpipe which she learned was called the epiglottis after becoming intimately familiar with touching it constantly, and her body complied. It was thin, pure liquid, all bile. This was when it burned the most.

She took in a sharp breath and coughed.

After spending more than an hour on this exhausting effort, she sat on the floor of the shower, the water gone cold. Feeling movement in her belly, she wondered if she got it all out, lamenting how it was so much easier to feel if her stomach was actually empty before the pregnancy. Now, all the motion in there distracted her, all the fluttering and twinges, the lurching, constant call of nausea, the shifting of her organs and the fatigue of growing life inside of her own still-growing body. She used to be able to feel even the small slosh of a gulp of water in the empty cavern of her shrunken stomach, and she'd do everything possible to keep it empty.

Despite the dizzying exhaustion, a calm enveloped her. Purging was her salvation. She reveled in the fact that even her body's needs for basic survival, its constant fight to live, or its threats to die, all of it was something she could just outwill.

Proof she could endure anything.

Lila stared blankly at the tub floor, and snapping into functioning, she fumbled for the shampoo bottle in a stupor, realizing it was time to wash her hair and soap herself, that she needed to brush her teeth, and get back to her research.

She let the water pour into her mouth, swished it around, and as she opened her eyes to spit, an enormous roach skittered up the shower tiles toward the ceiling.

"Get out!" she screamed at it, her voice a hoarse rasp and throat on fire. "Get away from me!"

She scrambled over the lip of the tub and frantically pulled a robe on, stuffing her wet arms through the sleeves and running out of the bathroom as fast as she could without slipping, her hair dripping all over the carpet.

"Mom!" she screamed. "Mom!"

"What?" Vivian called out from the distance of several rooms away, rushing down the hall. "Lila. You're getting everything wet."

Lila was already sobbing. "There's…there's…" Lila couldn't even say it, she was so disturbed. Vivian had a defeated expression on her face, one that knew what this was going to be about.

"Where is it?" Vivian said flatly, her voice groggy, rattled from being woken.

"A roach. In the shower." Lila wiped at her running nose. "I saw it when…" she doubled over and hyperventilated in bursts. "…When I was in there."

Vivian sighed. "Calm down. All right? I'll get it. I'm going to call an exterminator. Will that make you feel better?"

"Nothing will make it better! The exterminator won't be able to do anything!" Her labored breathing was getting worse, sharply punctuating between words. "He'll just kill a few of them," she gasped for air, "then more will come and they'll be furious!" Lila barked, taking another shallow breath and wiping away rivulets of tears. "It's pointless! Everything is pointless! They're coming back!" she yelled and stormed off to her bedroom, slamming the door behind her.

Lila had been reading a book about the resilience of cockroaches, and this made her paranoid that a colony of them could overthrow humanity with little effort, fearing how many were crawling up the drainpipes this second, how quickly they could be reproducing. She considered if she should pour bleach down the drains again. It seemed like even if she bathed in bleach, even if she drank the bleach, she wouldn't be able to get rid of the weight of everything, of the unwanted life inside of her, of the approaching inevitable.

In an attempt to ease her anxiety, Lila fumbled through the books on her bed, found the book about roaches, and immediately began reading. It calmed her, though only slightly.

Vivian barged through the door, wincing at the sight of her daughter surrounded by stacks of books and piles of papers.

"Just come out for breakfast, will you? You need to eat something. You've got to stop this, Lila. Get out of your head. There's no time for this anymore. You're going to be a mother soon. Mothers don't have time for this," she said, exasperated.

"I'll be right there," Lila said, not lowering her book.

The passage she was reading about cockroach eggs and incubation periods made her paranoid about the life growing inside her. It sickened her how fast insects could multiply, emerging out of just a tiny, fertilized egg. She remembered what her old biology teacher used to say about reproductive cycles, how a womb was a perfect habitat for growth. A warm place. A home. The ideal environment for many insects was anywhere dark, warm, or wet. She worried about them getting inside of her, finding warmth in her dark places, and this disturbed Lila deeply, even though she couldn't stop obsessing over it.

Now that she was pregnant, Lila regarded her body as a battleground. A kind of prison, trapped in a parasitic exchange with all nutrients draining from her, leaving her more vulnerable to when the swarms would attack. And she was more defenseless than usual, all this weight she had to lug around, making her slow. The perfect prey. That's what they wanted, to see her weak.

In a flash of panic, images from the nightmare visions came to Lila of the enormous spider with a grotesquely bloated body. In tonight's version of the dream, she'd squished it, then its slime oozed out and drowned her in a wave, filling her lungs with the guts, spilling out to terrorize the world. It reminded her of the giant peach the stop-motion boy had in that movie she loathed as a little girl, the one that gave her nightmares. She worried that insects the size of children, commuting via fruit, were anywhere at any time, watching from the sky.

"Lila! Now!" Vivian shouted from the kitchen.

Lila scoffed and carefully set her books down as she slid off the side of her bed, dragging her feet along like a lazy slug, dreading having to interact with her mother. Normally, she'd bring a book with her, but her mother freaked out if there were books at the table. And she didn't have the energy to argue.

Lila slowly crossed the hallway to the kitchen. Vivian poured herself a bowl of Cheerios, drenching the cereal in honey while squeezing that little plastic bear, the look and smell of it making Lila nauseous. She recalled the several times she'd stressed to Vivian that honey was bee vomit, unsuccessfully. Vivian hovered around the kitchen cabinet, guarding the honey as if she were its queen. "Do you want some?" she asked.

Lila shook her head no, just standing there at the crest of the dining room where the tile met the carpet. She wouldn't sit at the table. Her mother and food in the same room repulsed her. She remembered the times she found insects in her food, always in the presence of Vivian. Lila wondered if everything was her mother's fault. If somehow, Vivian was doing it intentionally, scattering bugs on plates like a garnish. Maybe it was her way of trying to make Lila snap out of it, some cruelty learned from Lila's father. Or Marcus.

Fighting the sour milk smell from across the room, Lila remembered a time from ages ago when she found a cricket in her milk. She knew she had mistakenly consumed dozens of bugs over the years, many of which crawled into her mouth while she slept—years' worth of them—but this dead cricket had traumatized her, the way it floated belly-up in the white liquid, its antennae in little hair-like wisps, that lifeless body, legs stiff.

The moment she had seen it, she spit the entire mouthful of milk back in the glass. Her tongue ran automatically along her teeth, dragging over the ridges of each tooth like some kind of feeler searching for chunks of the detached dead, for thin strings of antennae, pieces of a leg. She had immediately rushed to the sink to spit, gagged, and couldn't bear to pour out the glass because she worried the carcass would be sitting there in the drain forever, waiting for her, microscopic bits of it floating up with the dirty water whenever someone turned on the dishwasher.

"Are you not going to eat? You're being ridiculous," Vivian chastised. "You have to eat something. If your father were alive to see you like this…" she mumbled under her breath. "He would never forgive you. He would never forgive *me*. None of this would be happening."

Vivian almost started to cry and put a hand over her face, the one with half of her pinky amputated. Then she took a deep breath and rummaged around the cupboards, loudly slamming dishes around, pulling down the bowl with a small chip on the edge that Lila had put in it intentionally, to mark it. That clamoring of dishes irked her, especially the sight of that bowl.

This reminded her of another time, Lila remembered it well, when there was a spider in her broccoli chowder, its corpse lying in the very same bowl her mother held now, nearly the whole half of the spider missing. As if she had already consumed the first half, likely cut it straight down the middle with the spoon without realizing. That missing half must have stuck to a broccoli tree that slid down her esophagus, or broken apart into such tiny, minuscule pieces, that she imagined them as pepper flakes, and so she had unknowingly swallowed them, bit by bit, one centimeter at a time.

Vivian tried to start casual conversation, ignoring the tension between the two of them. "You think the baby will look like him, maybe get those adorable dimples?" she asked as she pulled a chair out and sat herself at the table, setting her bowl down, as well as the empty chipped bowl across from hers, for Lila.

Lila struggled to control her nausea, the burn of acid creeping up her throat.

"I don't think so," Lila responded, glancing at the photo on the fridge of her own infancy, baby curls winding around the top of her head like noodles. Marcus once told her noodles are skinny worms, after which Lila stopped eating noodles entirely.

"This baby will be nothing like Marcus."

When Marcus wasn't subjecting Lila to his antics, he was inflicting it on their high school classmates, or on the insects. She didn't know which was more upsetting, insects dead or alive. Even though it made no sense to Marcus, Lila wished he wouldn't kill them. But he liked to. He always laughed about it the same way he laughed when he made fun of Lila, just his sense of humor. Since Lila didn't have any friends or siblings, Marcus was all she had, though he was never particularly nice to her. She always tried to convince herself that maybe he didn't mean it, all the awful things he'd say.

"Your paint splotch is dark again," he'd let her know, referring to the mark on the back of her thigh. It made her want to stop wearing shorts altogether. The wine-colored patch of skin bloomed red like some kind of rash, and he'd laugh and call her a lobster. She thought it was more reminiscent of a ladybug or something seen on a Latrodectus spider, the strange red blotch so freakishly noticeable, though she never told anyone this. She always feared she got it from insects. Her mother said it was a birthmark. Lila didn't understand what a birthmark even was.

Vivian looked at her daughter before picking up her spoon. She bowed her head to silently pray, and Lila lowered hers too, but didn't close her eyes. This gesture was important to her mother, and it didn't bother Lila to do it. It was better than getting yelled at. Before she looked up, the sound of crunching cereal broke the silence.

"I've scheduled you an appointment with a therapist," Vivian said between bites as her spoon clanged against the bowl. "You'll see her today, right after school. It's time for all of this to be over."

Lila didn't ask about the appointment. She could only focus on trying to blur out the sight of the kitchen in her mind, and that bowl she would never dare use again, as it would always be: the graveyard for the spider.

II

THE SMALL ROOM was almost dark, with wilting plants in the corner casting shadows from the dim light of a lone gloomy window. The beige office couch contrasted the wood paneling that spanned an entire wall, darkening the space further.

"Miss Lila Morales, is it? Hello, Lila. My name is Nazaret, but here I'm Dr. Peralta. You can call me Dr. P if you want." The woman extended a hand, but Lila only stared at her skinny fingers.

Dr. Peralta had a thin needle nose, and Lila imagined her like a grasshopper or a locust, turning sandy brown or green, making horrifying sounds. The doctor crossed her legs and the scrape of her pants jolted like electricity through the air.

"Is it all right if I call you Lila? Or do you have a preferred name?"

"Just Lila," she said.

"Okay Lila, let me tell you a little about myself. I've been a psychotherapist for about seven years, and I love working with teens and young adults, even though I'm about two decades older than you," she smiled and then paused, studying Lila. "You know, I remember how stressful it was being your age. I can't imagine dealing with pregnancy on top of it. All those hormones!" She regarded Lila the way all adults did when they saw her, diminishing Lila's entire existence to just the current state of her body. "I'm glad you're here. Can you tell me more about you? About what brings you to see me and the symptoms you're experiencing?"

Lila maintained her usual stony expression, though she struggled to make eye contact. This doctor wasn't going to get it, so what was the point in sharing? She didn't answer the question.

Dr. Peralta blinked at Lila a few times in the lingering silence, waiting. "Well," she began slowly, "your mother tells me you aren't eating, and you're suffering from an insect phobia. Do you feel that defines your experience? I understand you've also lost someone close to you recently, the father of your baby. That must be difficult. Your mother tells me that it's only been two years since you've lost your own father as well."

Father would be a praying mantis, Lila thought, examining this doctor, how vulnerable and prey-like she seemed. Just another face in the scourge. *Father would eat her.*

Lila fidgeted, and goosebumps covered her arms. She thought some more of her dead father. How he never believed her either. How he would hate all of this. That he was surely rolling over in his casket in a rage, covered in maggots with worms writhing all over him, body lost to decay. She remembered the screaming fight where she begged her mom to cremate him, so he wouldn't get infested, left behind to become insect food.

She wondered if enough worms could fill his insides to control what physical matter was left of him, if they could overtake the gaping spaces of his remains with enough voracity to reanimate his corpse, and the writhing bug-zombie would break forth from beyond the grave and trudge all the way home to shatter the glasses in their kitchen in one of his fits, scream at Lila with worms crawling out of his mouth. And that's exactly what he'd do if he could see his daughter's big belly waddling into a therapist's office to talk about *feelings*. Making a public spectacle of it. She thought how if Marcus wasn't already dead, and her father wasn't already dead, he would have killed Marcus himself. But not before he killed her first. A pregnant, sixteen-year-old daughter? Not in their family.

Lila realized this therapist had been asking her questions and faded back into awareness of the present moment. She said what she always said whenever a doctor pretended to care. "I'm here because my mom made me come here. Because she doesn't believe me."

"Doesn't believe you about what?" Lila could tell that Dr. Peralta was already getting a slight tone in her voice, ready to defend Vivian. She began to write notes. The doctor's arms were too long, covered with her long-sleeved blouse that crept up too high above her wrists.

"That it's happening again, with the insects. They're everywhere. They're coming back, like the plagues. A lot of people are going to die."

"Everywhere? Where do you see them, specifically? Tell me about them. What makes you certain they are…returning, as you say?" Dr. Peralta had a puzzled expression on her face, a look that said, *Are you hearing what is coming out of your mouth? Does this not sound ridiculous to you?*

"It's been a prophetic theme throughout all of time. People just don't pay attention," Lila said.

"And how did you come to know this?" Dr. Peralta pressed her, sounding almost accusatory, still scratching at her notepad. Lila could already tell this woman was going to treat her like she was insane.

"Like I said," Lila was starting to get upset, but decided not to give the doctor the satisfaction. "It's written into all of recorded history."

Lila rolled her eyes before continuing and paused a moment. She shifted in her seat, looking at something in the corner of Dr. Peralta's office. "You ever heard of *The Mothman Prophecies*?" As Lila spoke, she watched a moth fluttering around inside the corner lampshade, irked by the tiny noise of it hitting against the light bulb.

"That moth over there now," Lila pointed. "It's an omen."

"Oh?" Dr. Peralta remarked, with blatant disinterest, not lifting her gaze from her notes. "Tell me, when did you learn of this prophecy, and of this *moth* man?" She said it like it was the name of a superhero or Disney character, completely missing the overwhelming dread that Lila felt even in speaking its name.

It upset Lila when adults dismissed her. How they believed they knew more than her, that whatever she said must be wrong because she was young. That her age negated every experience she had. That their arrogance always outweighed empathy.

So, Lila made the doctor wait again before she answered, as a small punishment. She stood up, very bothered by the moth, almost frantic. She pulled a novel out of her purse and gently set it down before aggressively digging for her black light flashlight. Once she found it, she switched it on and scanned the room, every crack and ridge in the floorboards. She spent a considerable amount of time with the couch, panicked she had not checked it for crawling things before sitting down. She made her way over to the window, holding her belly, and looked out over the edge of the windowsill wondering what it would be like to leap and float, little paper-thin wings holding her, gliding around, chalky and light.

"I've just always known," Lila finally said in a soft voice.

Lila was suddenly reminded of Exodus 10, where God sent the plague of locusts to Egypt, and then another time in third grade, when her teacher, Mrs. Crenshaw, kept a live scorpion trapped inside a glass tank. Watching the scorpion each morning made Lila certain it would get out, start crawling after her, wait flat in the crack between the carpet and the door jamb, strike at any moment. She thought of masses of them, their pincers and stingers coming for her. She thought of the women of Egypt crying, locusts shrieking.

The idea was to prove that scorpions could live for an eternity without food, so they never fed it, just watched it slowly waste away, waiting to die. The only time it moved was when Mrs. Crenshaw threw another scorpion in there with it, and the class was invited to watch the two cannibalize each other. Marcus thought the fight was representative of humanity, of the world.

There he was, invading her thoughts again. As if in response, the back of her thigh burned. Lila scratched at her birthmark and paced beside the couch, trying to quiet the intrusion.

Dr. Peralta didn't comment on Lila's pacing, or on the book, and proceeded with an array of questions. "How have you been coping since losing your boyfriend? Let's talk about that. Do you feel…abandoned? Especially after the death of your father?" Dr. Peralta's eyeglasses slid slightly down the bridge of her nose, her eyes eerily piercing.

"I don't know. It's like my father was dead even before he died," Lila said.

"Hmmm," Dr. Peralta said and nodded, furrowing her brow in reaction to this. "What was your relationship like?"

Lila shrugged, unsure how to answer. "He wanted a son. But he got me instead."

Dr. Peralta waited for Lila to elaborate. When she didn't, she asked, "And your boyfriend?"

Lila did not want to talk about Marcus. She didn't know what she was supposed to say. Even though she missed Marcus sometimes, she knew larger factors were at work, things he wouldn't understand. Things she herself didn't understand. Dr. Peralta waited for something, anything.

"Would you say his absence causes you to worry more about the insects?" Dr. Peralta tried again.

Lila pondered this. "It helped when Marcus listened, but it doesn't make me worry more. The worry is always there. It never leaves. The insects are my first memory. My pre-memories. I don't know how to make anyone believe me, that they really are coming. It's going to be soon. I can hear them buzzing in my ears."

Dr. Peralta scratched at her own ear, as if she heard it, that same buzz.

She wrote something else down, almost racing to keep the thought. "We are going to come back to that comment about your first memory. But for now, tell me, Lila, do you ever see or hear things you aren't sure where they came from—words or voices, images?"

Lila winced but did not answer.

"Do you ever lose gaps of time? For example, do you enter a room and find you can't remember why you came in there, or even that you had entered the room at all? Maybe you don't remember putting on the clothes you're wearing, or how it's suddenly a certain time of day?"

Lila wasn't sure what she was getting at, probably trying to diagnose her with something to refute her, reasoning that she was ill, therefore, incorrect. These constant battles were one thing that made Marcus special to Lila. Marcus was the only one who ever took this seriously.

"And perhaps this worry interferes with your everyday life, like how you avoid many foods because of concerns with the insects? Or is it something more?"

"Sure, yeah." Lila only nonchalantly agreed about avoiding foods. She was not going to say anything about the bulimia. Lila hated doctors, all of their questions. If they knew she was bulimic, especially while pregnant, they'd want her to stop. They'd try to *make her* stop. Even whenever Lila convinced herself she'd never do it again, she still needed to throw up, to get everything out.

"Do you find yourself feeling dark thoughts about your baby? Any thoughts of harming your baby? Of harming yourself?"

Lila smiled at that question. She cradled her belly and said exactly what this doctor wanted to hear. "I would never do that."

Dr. Peralta did not express any reaction, as if she had to ask this question multiple times a day and wanted to move past it. "Okay, I'm going to send you home with some assessments, and before we go, I have some homework for you. I would like you to start a journal about your insect experiences. Eventually we will start a food log, but let's take this one step at a time, since your phobia seems to drive your anxiety with food. Can you do that for me? Whenever you see a bug, or feel afraid of them, I want you to write it down. And if you feel comfortable, we'll discuss some of the entries at the start of our sessions. How does that sound?"

"That's fine," Lila said flatly. She didn't want to seem too eager, but she was excited by this idea. Now she could document them. Track them. Why hadn't she been doing this all along? Yes, this would go nicely with her research routine. She could get closer to timing the return.

She knew which journal she'd use to write in. One of Marcus's old notebooks that she didn't have the strength to throw away. One she had stolen from his backpack, his name scrawled on the inside cover in his chicken scratch. He'd written a few equations in it from an old math class, but almost all of the pages were blank otherwise. She loved his sloppy handwriting, even though she could barely read it. Just like her own.

Fluttering across her peripheral vision outside the office window, a butterfly flew by and perched on a branch. Lila's eyes followed it, and then she got up to look, walking over to the sill.

"Are you all right, Lila? Do they also upset you? Butterflies?"

Lila watched it intently. She pressed her fingertips against the glass so tightly that the tension formed white halos at the top of her fingers, interrupting the circulation. Her unpainted nails were bitten down to the skin.

She could feel the doctor's eyes on the back of her head, poring into her. The silence was uncomfortable, but Lila didn't care about making people uncomfortable. She believed her role in this world was to be a messenger. Not anyone's friend.

"I don't know," Lila finally said, breathing so close to the glass, it fogged. "I almost think they're trying to offset the moths."

III

AFTER SURVIVING THE last appointment of the day, Dr. Nazaret Peralta was drowning in unfinished paperwork. She glanced at that moth slamming itself against the bulb under the lampshade and wondered how it could be anything more than a moth, surely not some symbol of doom. Lila might call this moth prophetic, Nazaret wouldn't dare call it anything.

She looked at her watch, already nine o'clock. She had to stay late for an emergency session, a client whose mother had just been murdered, and she was still reeling from the stress.

Rushing through her notes, her phone rang, and she fished it out of her desk drawer, seeing her friend Jess's name on the screen. Before she could even say hello, Jess blurted, "Hi Naz, sorry to call late. Can you talk?"

"Hi! Yeah, I'm just about to leave the office."

"Okay, are you sitting down?"

"Why? What happened?" Nazaret's heart sank, paranoid. "Is it the kids?"

"No. Everyone's fine. Just sit down. I have something to show you. It's going to be difficult to see, okay? I'm sending you a picture. Let me know when you get it."

There was a pause on the line, noises of tapping on a screen, a chime sound.

When the photo appeared, Nazaret's familiar heartache swelled. It was of her husband Gabe at an upscale restaurant, with a beautiful, younger woman. The one he'd had his most recent affair with. Blonde, thin, lanky, girl-next-door. Everything Nazaret wasn't.

"No," Nazaret said out loud, trying to convince herself. "That's from six months ago. He ended this."

"I saw him with my own eyes. I just took this tonight!"

"It's old!" Nazaret snapped. "It has to be!"

"Naz," Jessica said. "He's a liar. Now you finally have proof."

"That picture is old," Nazaret repeated, certain now that this was a mistake. "We've been talking about having another baby anyway."

Jess sighed, trying to avoid a fight. "Yeah, so he can keep you locked down. Make you forget what he did. What he's still doing. Just leave him, Naz."

"What are you talking about? Things are fine. They're finally a lot better, actually. Besides, I don't have time for a divorce right now."

"Are you planning on keeping up this charade the rest of your life? You're miserable."

"I'm fine."

"No, you're in denial. He's never been good to you."

Nazaret became teary-eyed, more out of embarrassment than sadness. "But loyalty means something to me. Vows mean something to me."

"Loyalty to what? Where's your loyalty to yourself? What about to me? We've been friends since we were kids! Why would you believe him over me?" Jess started to raise her voice in frustration, then quieted again. "I'm telling you, Nazaret, staying with him will be your biggest regret."

"I highly doubt that."

"Maybe not now. Maybe not even in five years. But when you've wasted your entire life with Gabe because you can't face reality, you'll wish you listened to me. Because you know what's going to happen? You'll ignore this until more years pass and you and I are having this conversation yet again, same as we did five years ago when you were sobbing to me through your first pregnancy, when you caught Gabe the first time. It will get worse. He might leave you for some twenty-year-old and you have a breakdown. Just kick him out."

"I have kids," Nazaret said. "I can't just get divorced."

"Why not? You have the money. You've given enough of your life to him. For what?"

"I love him," Nazaret said.

"You don't. You love the idea of him. The potential. You're a fixer. He's eternally broken. He's not one of your clients. Not everyone can be helped. Not everyone wants to be. What are you so afraid of? Your life not looking good on paper? You are the modern woman, you think you have it all. But you have nothing! It's an illusion. You're working yourself to death, taking care of everyone else—your clients, your kids, a man who treats you like trash. You're talking about another baby like that's going to distract you from how deeply you've buried everything he's done to you. Enough."

"I can't..." Nazaret shook her head, unable to process this conversation.

"He's still cheating! And he cheated on you while you were pregnant!" she yelled.

"You think about that more than I do!" Nazaret shouted back. "That's in the past."

"Because I actually love you! And I'm the one who has to see you cry, to put you back together. I'm the one you shelve while you let him hurt you, but I'm the one who is always here. In the past? This is now! At what point are you going to see this for what it is? Leave him!" she yelled into the phone, and Nazaret pulled the phone away from her ear. "Please, I'm begging you. He's changed you. You're a shell. I miss my friend. I'm worried about you. Please, Naz." She said this with heartbreaking sincerity, her voice almost breaking into a cry.

Nazaret felt like she was about to cry, too. But she shoved it down, refusing to allow it. She rationalized this all was a mistake. Jess in detective mode, digging up an old photo online. Nazaret began pacing, not listening anymore, tuning out everything Jess was still saying. She looked at the stack of papers beside her, lamenting the time, realizing she needed to get home. The framed family portrait on her desk with Gabe and her children loomed in the corner.

"Look, I have to go. Thank you for your concern, but mind your own fucking business." She hung up, then blocked Jess's number. If she had to choose between grieving a friend or ripping apart her family, she decided cutting the friend would be easier.

Nazaret took a deep breath and closed her eyes, letting this float away into some vaulted space in her brain, with the rest of her suffering she left untouched and did not have room to address. She felt simultaneously filled with devastation and misplaced rage, deciding this was a malicious act from Jessica. Then the anger became a hollowness, leaving her gutted and empty.

In a sudden awareness that she had a body, she realized she was ravenous. By the time she got home, everyone would be in bed, and she was so exhausted that she wanted to shovel food in her mouth immediately and go right to sleep.

She decided on fast food and almost felt guilty because she didn't allow her kids to eat this type of garbage. After inhaling the burger and large order of fries, she found she was pulling into her driveway.

Having dissociated the whole drive, she barely even remembered going through the drive-thru line. First she was consumed by her anger, then overtaken with the events of her clients' lives. It had to be the way her last client described every gory detail of how her mom had been bashed over the head with a hammer until she slowly bled out to death on their living room tile, then there was that pregnant girl who couldn't stop talking about bugs, and her longtime client who kept picking at a scab on his knee while he talked about his childhood neglect. The sight of him doing this made her want to pick off all of her own skin and start over.

She put the key into the front door and quietly snuck down the hall. She assumed the kids were asleep, as the lumps on their beds resembled their forms. When she opened her bedroom door, the bedroom was dark, the only light from a moon ray shining in through the curtainless eyelid dormer.

Gabe did not wait up, and she crept into their bed beside him, sound asleep, and shoved up against the crack of the wall. She did not dare let herself examine him for evidence of what she saw in the photograph. Marks on his neck, lipstick on his collar. She didn't look. He snored, and she wanted to hold his nose closed. Opening the nightstand drawer for one of her orange prescription bottles, she shook two white pills into her palm and swallowed them.

She drifted to sleep.

At two in the morning, she jolted awake in a strange stir. She had chills and shuddered, as if a languid fly had landed on her and was trying to crawl into her ears, so she attempted to shoo it as the buzz in her head grew more persistent. *What is happening to me? Tinnitus? Am I getting sick?*

She slid out from the comforter to walk to the bathroom, eyes barely cracked open, and caught a blurry glimpse of an enormous praying mantis perched against the glass as she passed by the window. The mantis squared its ferocious arms, clutched a small lizard in its claws, and bit off its head.

Nazaret shuddered at the sight of this, her ears blaring with a ringing, that same buzz from earlier. She fumbled around the medicine cabinet for ear drops, fighting an overwhelm of dizziness, when an unusual noise frightened her.

Faintly at first, she heard a croaking sound her children had never made before, and disoriented, still half asleep, she rushed out of the room, clambering all over the house searching for them. With their beds empty, their doors ajar, she shouted their names. But no one responded. Gabe slept on. There was only that eerie noise emanating throughout the house.

She followed the sound, tracking their cacophony of shrieks to behind the pantry door. The shelves were empty, nothing left, only crumbs scattered on the tile.

She found them at last, her babies. They sat together, in seemingly perfect health, different but the same. There were little ridges all over their legs, miniature lumps like teeth sticking out. Their shins were longer than she remembered, knees pointy and extended, feet stretched out and thin. They turned their heads toward her in alarming unison and opened their mouths to let out a scraping locust song, stridulating with shaking croaks that made her jump in surprise.

AFTER A FEW hours of godawful sleep, Nazaret fumbled through her skincare routine and washed her face, disgusted by the sight of the smeared remnants of her lipstick. It was like she had new, strange mouthparts that no longer fit the outline of her natural lips. Somehow, she had forgotten to wash her makeup off last night.

Her piercing eyes looked back at her. A blackness inside of the blackness reflected back. She remembered how she hated those black eyes as a teenager, when being blonde and tall and impossibly thin was the mainstream beauty standard, when she used to think her black eyes were ugly. When no one sang love songs about girls with black eyes. How she would hope to wake up and have hazel eyes, blue eyes, packs of eyes. Anything else.

Packs of eyes? She laughed at herself. *What a weird thought.*

She walked into the kitchen, readying herself to make everyone breakfast. Her son emerged from the hallway, scratching at his head.

Oh god, she thought, the fear creeping in. "Come here, sweetheart," she told him and combed his hair down with her fingers. Her throat dropped into her stomach as she parted a few strands of his hair, examining his scalp. There they were, teeny insects crawling around, her dread confirmed. Lice.

She remembered her own childhood experience with lice, the bloodsuckers finding perfect sanctuary in her tumultuous waves when she shared a hair tie with Marcy Ortega at Jennifer Hilton's birthday party. They all did a hair-brushing train and then braided each other's hair. "Stupid girl shit," her brother had called it. "No wonder you got lice," he'd smirked at her. But then he got lice, too, and she delighted in this karmic vengeance. Their mother had been furious. It took them a week to completely clean out their apartment and get rid of them. She dreaded this moment, being on the other side of it. The parent side. Dreading how she was going to have to spend every spare moment the next few days washing all of their clothes, bedding, brushes, the couch, everything. Children were little subways of contagion.

Fumbling around the bathroom cabinet for lice shampoo, she felt like she'd been hit by a truck. Exhaustion clouded her, and God, she was hungry. And pissed at Gabe. Was he seriously still asleep? The hunger almost blotted out every other sight and thought in her head, a groaning emptiness of her hollow insides. Even the sight of bloodthirsty insects ravaging her child's scalp didn't deter the hunger.

Trying not to let her stomach turn, she tore the shampoo boxes open impatiently and sat her son down on the closed toilet lid. She pulled vinyl gloves on and slathered her own hair with an entire bottle of Nix and swished it into a mound at the top of her head, securing it with a clip. Then she applied the product to his hair and began combing with that fine-toothed nit comb, keeping close attention to the scalp. She had already discovered several eggs that were now gunking up the tiny teeth of the comb, and when she found hatchlings of a few live lice, her stomach lurched. Filthy little parasites, trying to prey on her baby.

Parting his hair at his nape, she found several more latched on, sucking his blood. "I did your hair yesterday morning before school. There's no way I missed this." *Oh my God, how are there so many?* She realized she didn't really remember yesterday morning. How last night even was hazy. Did she have a bad dream? Why couldn't she remember? Were the kids playing in the pantry?

She smiled at him, trying to hide her disgust. He raised a hand to his scalp to scratch.

"It itches," he said in a whine and squirmed as she scolded him more harshly than she intended.

"No!" and grabbed at his hand with her left hand that was not wielding the comb. "Sorry, sweetheart, you can't scratch right now. Okay? Here I'll comb. Better?"

She scraped at his scalp with the comb, wanting to vomit at the hordes of lice, their eggs, their endlessness. How did they reproduce so quickly? What would her daughter's hair be like? Probably worse. Were they all completely infested? Would they have to burn down the house? Were lice crawling all over her right now? Were they leaving empty nits in all of her combs and brushes? Were there full-grown lice gallivanting through her long hair, falling into her shirt?

She shuddered, and felt very itchy herself, wanting to dig her hands into her mound of hair piled on top of her head and drag her nails against her scalp until it bled. She wanted to rip off her clothes, to stand under hot water in the shower and scrape—no—peel off her skin with more than a comb. With a blade. To shed this old, dirty skin, an exoskeleton she'd outgrown. Anything to make the gritty, tormented feeling go away.

She almost had that same insatiable itch she'd had as a teenager, wanting to cut. She remembered being desperate for a way to justify this behavior to herself, reading up about bloodletting, that cutting wasn't some weird modern problem, or even a her problem, that humanity had always wanted to exsanguinate them-selves. *Where did that come from?* she thought. *It's all this chaos bringing up old anxiety*, she rationalized to herself, the therapist in her soothing away the shock of this, not allowing herself to acknowledge her inner turmoil from Jess's call that she was pretending never happened.

She moved to the next section, focused, made sure to get the lice all combed out. It made her feel sick. That's when she thought she heard a voice.

You can kill us, but we'll just come back. We outnumber you. We'll always outnumber you. We breed so quickly. We're endless. You'll never kill us all.

Startled, she dropped the comb, not reacting as it fell over the porcelain lip and clanked against the bottom of the empty tub.

Her son turned to her and said, "Mommy, you dropped it."

The trail of his words were muffled, distorted, and his face swirled into something disfigured, the coppery tone of his skin changing color to the grayish-red of one of their monstrous louse faces. His features transformed into itty bitty eyes, his mouth now a gaping, ferocious maw, looking to feast. To feast on her.

"Mommy?" The thing that used to be her son said. "Mommy?" it kept repeating.

It was looking at her. It wanted to suck her blood. To latch on and never let go. To drain the life out. She suddenly had a flash of this disgusting thing at her breast, biting and slurping for years-gone milk, then crawling atop her head and gnawing her scalp, hunting for blood.

Her phone vibrated in her pocket, and she gasped, breaking the trance of her son's disfigured face that now appeared perfectly normal. The vibrating sensation almost felt as if it howled from inside of her, a whirring trapped within. It was her alarm. She had twenty minutes to get ready and leave for work.

She handed her son her phone to play with and rushed to pour a mug of coffee for Gabe. She stood at the side of the bed, nudging his shoulder.

"Gabe," she said. "Please get up. The kids." She stood there for a minute, waiting to make sure his eyes were permanently open, before hurrying back to the bathroom to rinse out her son's hair, then her own. After frantically checking her head and finding nothing, she sloppily braided her wet hair and threw on a cardigan, rushing out the door.

On the drive, the roads were congested, at a near standstill. Her hands shook, sitting in traffic. She did not want to deal with her clients. She did not want to deal with anything. All she could think about was how hungry she was. A low-grade panic was steadily rising to the top of her throat, burning through her esophagus, thrumming through her fingertips. Her whole body seemed to be ringing. The other faces in the cars next to hers looked exactly like hers—as urgent, desperate, ready. Swarming all over the roads, the cities. Infesting the world. She could drive through the barrier right now, fly off the edge of the overpass. Never have to live on this earth again. No more of Gabe's bullshit. No more kids with lice. No more clients with fucked-up lives and unsolvable problems. No more anything. She'd be free.

Or she could wait for the cars to keep on inching at a crawl, for authorities to clear the accident or whatever the hell was clogging everything up, and for the masses to scuttle along, patiently scrabbling to get through. Then once the traffic cleared, she could gun it straight into the wheat field ahead, pedal to the floor. That's what she should do. Drive into that field and feast.

Someone honked behind her, screaming expletives and pointing at the clearing roadway. She hadn't been paying attention and tapped the gas pedal to move ahead with the line. Picking up speed, she saw the field of wheat pass her by, so open, inviting.

IV

NAZARET SHIFTED IN her office chair and gathered up her notes, trying to put herself in therapist mode, trying not to think about the chaos of the last week, of any remnants of lice she may have missed while cleaning over the weekend, or of the six-car pileup on the freeway last Friday that she could have died in but didn't. She checked her watch, patiently waiting for Lila to situate herself on the couch across from her as she opened her journal. She was surprised by the journal Lila chose, some old bent composition notebook that had clearly once belonged to her boyfriend. Lila appeared controlled, orderly, a girl who treated her books with devotion. This book? Couldn't have been hers. Nazaret didn't comment on this, but noted it.

Lila stared at the page and took a deep breath. "I should preface this by saying," she announced to Nazaret with enthusiasm, "we've been getting wasps, and it's making me feel panicked, I *have to* keep them away."

This change in Lila's demeanor surprised Nazaret, how she spoke freely, her eagerness to share. Nazaret realized if she wanted to get this girl talking, she had to center these delusions with insects.

Lila cleared her throat, her mousy voice only a little louder now. "I'm being haunted by wasps— Oh wait," she interrupted herself. "*Hunted?* I'm not sure. I can't read my handwriting. I'm being…haunted by wasps. I covered the whole patio with Pine Sol and cinnamon. It's supposed to deter them. Now I'm constantly revolted because the smell reminds me of insects. Mom gets mad when I do this, but I can't stop. I panic if they're near the windows. Even after I covered the patio, I could still see one of the wasps whirring around. It won't leave. It's hanging upside down from the patio roof, building a nest right outside my bedroom window. They're after me." She closed the journal and set it on her lap.

"I also stayed up all night disinfecting the windowsills and coating the glass with Windex," she added, as if just remembering. "I don't know if it helps, but I do it anyway. Last night, I also poured the rest of the Pine Sol down the drains. I poured enzymatic drain cleaner down too. Nothing works. I pour bleach, boiling water, baking soda with vinegar, and still they come."

"How often does this happen? That your sleep becomes disturbed?" Nazaret asked.

Lila shrugged, as if to suggest, *all the time.* "A lot. Even if I do sleep, I'll dream of them. I mean, I have visions of them. So I don't like to sleep because then I can't escape. If I'm asleep, I can't check to make sure they're not crawling on me. Sleep means I'm vulnerable. And they know that. That's when they'll try to come."

Nazaret wrote, *Paranoia causing sleep disturbances. Frequent nightmares. Poor, inconsistent sleep patterns.* Nazaret's hand started cramping, and she scanned over the several pages of comments she already had written down for Lila. There was so much that she almost didn't know where to start. Potential eating disorder, teenage pregnancy, dead boyfriend, dead father, strained mother relationship, apocalypse delusions, insect phobia.

"Last time we saw each other, you mentioned something about your first memory. Would you mind sharing it with me?"

"Actually, it's not a memory," Lila corrected. "It's a vision, like I said. It's something that *will* happen. Soon."

Nazaret kept writing. *Hallucinations? Pre-psychosis symptomology? Schizoaffective?*

"Tell me more about that. At what age did you first start having this *vision*—you've experienced this multiple times?"

"I don't know. Maybe four or five. It's the first time I can remember seeing this spider. I've seen that same spider many times since… In the visions."

"The same one?" Nazaret tried to keep her tone unbiased as she wrote down, *Major Depressive Disorder—Moderate— with psychotic features.*

"The vision is always the same. I'm alone in my room, then all of these insects come for me in a massive swarm. Sometimes they shatter the glass, flying through my window in droves. It's why I'm afraid of windows. Why I feel like I have to keep checking them. I don't know if that's the part that will come true, them finding me near a window. Other times, there's this buzzing that roars from inside the walls, then they come raining down the vents.

"And there's one part that never changes, this spider. This…enormous spider." Lila had a repulsed expression on her face, as if this was painful for her to describe. "It's a black widow. Its spinnerets are rushing, spinning a web, and I'm watching it, in a trance or something. The red on its abdomen looks like liquid, deep red, like it's drenched in blood, and the blood is dripping all over the web. The web is chaos—erratic, patternless, messy. Like all black widow webs, but this one, with the blood all over it, it looks like a glob of flesh, or something dead. So the spider just keeps spinning, building a barrier around itself. Protecting itself. Like it's preparing to lay eggs. Like it knows what's coming.

"In the last dream, I smashed it, which I would never do, and this fluid came out of it that filled up the room. I don't think it was venom. I don't know what it was. But I was in this sudden, overwhelming pain. Like I said, I don't think I was envenomated, but—

"Envenomated?"

"Yeah, injected with venom. But I couldn't breathe. My lungs were filling with something, like I was suffocating. My chest started burning. I felt hot. I felt like I was on fire. Then the whole room went black. I woke up and somehow knew I had died. That it killed me."

"Hmm, that sounds very disturbing." Nazaret said as she pushed her glasses back up the bridge of her nose. "I must say, though, I'm confused. What part of this comes across as a vision to you? It's not that I'm doubting you, but I would like to hear your thoughts."

"What do you mean?" Lila looked angry. She explained her reasoning as if there was a comprehension issue, not any other reason. "There are these swarms outside—" Lila lifted her hands, gesturing with large sweeping motions to illustrate the magnitude of this. "They break into my room, and it's obvious they've come to kill me. That they're going to kill everyone. It's happened before in history. Like I said, with the plagues. It will happen again. It's only a matter of time."

"I see," Nazaret said. "Can you describe for me where this all fits into your eating habits?"

Lila's eyes widened in annoyance. "Obviously I'm afraid of them getting in my food. And I'm sick all the time. I'm constantly nauscous."

Nazaret wrote, *Poor, inconsistent eating patterns. Possibly developing eating disorder.*

"Do you have a favorite food?"

"Not really. I mean, I don't know." Lila started to get defensive, agitated. "It doesn't really matter, I get sick all the time like I said, regardless of what I eat."

"In addition to our sessions, I might refer you to my colleague who is a fantastic psychiatrist, and there are several medications we can try that may help you."

"I don't need to be on drugs!" Lila spat. "Besides, my mom would never let me. She thinks God will fix me, or you will. She doesn't want me to take anything because of the baby. She barely lets me have Tylenol. That's why she's making me come here."

"Sounds like you have some animosity about that. Does your mother force you to participate in her religion?"

"My parents have always been very traditional Catholics. She's Irish-American, and my father was Mexican, from Nogales. He came to the United States just before they met. Catholicism was the one thing they agreed on."

"Oh!" Nazaret lit up, "My parents are from Hermosillo. My husband too. That's so cool that we have that connection! You know," she laughed, "my tata used to insist I was meant to be a curandera. I found my path to healing, just in a different way than he envisioned. You actually remind me of him. I think he would have liked you. I can see the same grit in you. He had what he called 'the sight', too. He was a good man. Always wanting to help people, to make the world better. I miss him."

"Thank you," Lila said and smiled a shy smile, maybe the first genuine smile Nazaret had seen. She wanted to relate to this child, but didn't know how to tell her that she too understood this burden. The weight of being responsible for guiding other people's fates at all times.

"Lila, I want to help you feel better, so you can experience life without all of this struggle. Are you ready to make some changes to see improvements?"

"I just don't think anything will help. Nothing can change what's coming."

"Depression is like that, an invasion of our whole being. Little bits of ourselves are consumed until there's nothing left we recognize. The former 'us' seems eaten away, gone forever, lost to a before-time. Or maybe to a time we've never known because this is how it's always been. And that's okay, Lila. It's okay. It's important for you to know you're not alone."

"But I *am* alone," Lila said. "Marcus is gone. You don't believe me. No one believes me."

"That's not—" Nazaret tried to say before Lila interjected. As a woman of science, a health professional, her job was to remain objective, clinical.

"And besides," Lila went on, "Everyone is always alone. We live alone. We die alone. We are alone. It's how it works," she said sharply.

"Soon, you will have your baby. Right now, you are less alone than you will ever be. You are sharing your body with another. Life is growing within you. That is amazing, isn't it?"

Lila said nothing to this and stared at the floor, reverting to her detachment defense that Nazaret had seen their first session.

Nazaret tried another angle with Lila. "Well, they do serve a purpose, if you think about it. The insects, I mean. For instance, we need insects for their job as nature's waste removal. Feasting on the dead, for example."

Lila's face scrunched up in disgust at this comment. "They're not here…for their *purpose*. Life doesn't exist for service. Even Marcus knew that. That's a grotesque thing to say. You know, we're a cruel species. The way we impose, decide what other species must do for us, kill at will. It's us who have no purpose. They know that. They're trying to get rid of us. We are the parasites."

Nazaret kept listening, analyzing, writing. *Entomophobia. Existential disturbances.*

"That's a very dark view on humanity. Do you have trouble trusting people?'

"Yes. Though I mean it, like, as a species. We are bad. All we do is kill."

"Quite a generalization, don't you think? Not everyone hurts others."

"You're not listening to what I'm saying," Lila said, raising her voice slightly. "We've gone too far. The return is almost here." Lila clutched the journal in her lap, comforted by its presence.

"It must be difficult, being young, witnessing the destruction of nature, all the collapse of our time. I imagine it's hard for someone your age to feel optimistic about the future. Do you feel responsible for the state of the world? That's a lot to put on yourself. You're only one person, after all."

"I feel responsible for what I know, that I have to get people to listen. It's like I'm screaming from inside a well, waiting to die, but no one hears me. Like I'm fated for this, for these… terrible things. That what I've done is…" she trailed off.

Nazaret looked at this poor, confused teenager, lost in grief. "What is it you've done? You can't punish yourself for what is outside of your control."

"Nothing. I—I just mean that… I don't know what I mean."

"Lila, when we experience loss, it's common for us to blame ourselves. But you are not responsible for the tragedies that have happened to you."

"I just hate feeling out of control, not being safe anywhere, in my own body. I'm constantly checking everything, on edge, anxious about ways they can get in, come near me. My food, my mouth, my clothes, my hair, my shoes, my underwear. I'm afraid that they're going to crawl inside of me."

"That's called hypervigilance. In a constant fear-state. It's our brain's survival strategy."

Lila started biting her nails, considering this. "You'd think I'd be better about it by now. That I'd be tougher."

"Why do you say that?"

"It's what everyone wants from me. Between my parents insisting I'd grow out of it, everyone at school harassing me, and Marcus, especially him. He was the opposite extreme. He tried to force me to face them, but I only got better at hiding my fear."

"Are you concerned about what others want of you? What do you mean he forced you?"

"Sometimes. And I don't know. He'd put me through these tests. He'd catch cockroaches and put them in my backpack just to see what I would do. Or he'd do this weird whistling thing, buzzing his lips together to sound like a fly, trying to condition me to the noise. He was really good at catching flies. But it was cockroaches he liked to torment me with most. Whenever he held one, a wave of nausea would consume me—seeing it in his palm, its armored body, folded wings, antennae twitching. I'd try to leave, but he'd grip my arm and pull me back. Then he'd bring it right up to my face and command me to look at it.

"'We've got to prepare you. You need to be able to look at them,' he'd say. 'You think you're going to last the return if you spend your whole life closing your eyes? You think you'll survive? Fucking look at it, Lila! You have to be able to kill them! To defend yourself.'

"Then, if I resisted, or tried to cover my face, he'd hold the roach over my head and scream at me. 'Look, Lila! Look at it!'" Lila started to shout, mimicking his intensity.

She stopped for a minute, quieting back to her usual, shy voice, realizing how loud she had gotten. "When I still wouldn't, he'd threaten to drop it in my hair. Drunk with fear, I'd flutter an eye open, my throat tingling with acid, like it was going to swell and close, like tiny legs were crawling up the filmy layer of my esophagus and threatening to march out in droves. Like my insides were filled with angry gnats battering around, pressing up in clouds against my lungs. I worried my heart would give out, that my body would fail at any moment.

"Finally, he'd laugh, like the whole thing was an enormous joke, like I was so dramatic for freaking out. Then he'd interlace his hands and squeeze his palms together as tight as he could, to crush it. Sometimes they wouldn't die, and he'd have to step on them.

"I thought for a time that I envied him, his bravery. Then I realized, he was never brave. He was never anything." Lila kept her gaze fixed, staring out the window.

"What you've just described is abusive. Was he aggressive with you in other ways? Any additionally menacing or troubling behaviors?" Nazaret examined Lila with questioning eyes, raising an eyebrow. She wrote down, *conduct disorder—boyfriend*?

"I mean, he never hit me. He was just scary sometimes."

Nazaret wanted to press her on this comment, but decided to let Lila continue.

"When I finally got to the point that I could look, that's when he'd try to make me touch them. He told me there was a lot of things in the world to be afraid of, but I could be brave if I wanted. That I didn't have to feel fear if I chose not to.

"This obsession with testing me got worse, over time. Marcus had been wanting to have sex with me, it's basically all he'd talk about besides the return. He'd do his usual routine, saying this same speech about fear over and over.

"I guess the first time I ever felt afraid of him was when he acted like he was doing a fear exercise with me, only he didn't have any insects to test me with. Instead, he unzipped his pants and kissed me, gripped the back of my head and pulled my face toward him. He told me to look. Just look. Then he grabbed my hand, and he told me to touch him, to be brave, that I could do anything I wanted in this world if I was brave."

V

LILA PULLED A book out of her backpack, *Bloody, Bloody, Curse and Spell, Leeches are The Cure from Hell: An Examination of Medieval Era Bloodletting* by a Dr. Willard Irving, entomologist and researcher, published by some obscure university press. She rummaged around looking for a pen. One of her notebooks had a pen trapped in the wire spiraling, and she struggled, digging her finger into the coil, trying to rescue it.

Situating the bloodletting book inside of her biology textbook to disguise it, she scanned through the first page of the third chapter—a section about the use of leeches for blood cleansing. She almost had to skip past the anatomical diagrams of leech bodies and details of how they feasted upon those with various ailments or diseases. It made her think how sad it was that when people were suffering, they could be taken advantage of so easily. The way parasites fed under the guise of being there to help. How people believed the craziest things just to be saved.

She imagined the leeches drinking gallons of blood, the filth of covering oneself in disease-bearing insects intentionally. But she was intrigued by the concept that humans could be *bad in the blood*. She thought on this. Maybe that was something to note. She wrote it down with the pen she finally freed from her notebook. "Genetic connection? Familial? Bad…blood?" *That could make sense*, she admitted to herself. *Maybe it really is all my mother's fault.*

"Lila, come up to my desk, please," the substitute called out while everyone was quietly working on assignments. Lila hated being singled out. She was embarrassed already, even just having to walk to the front of a room where everyone would be looking at her, probably staring at her belly.

"This is not a current event," he said as he held up Lila's essay outlining an article about a new breed of oversized wasp, with alarming volumes of swarms coming in from overseas.

"Yes it is. It's about—"

"Look, it's not my rule, but you know the policy. Must center people or events."

Lila rolled her eyes and began to head back to her desk, realizing she was going to have to spend the entire period redoing her homework.

"Oh, and one more thing," he said, and when Lila turned, he tried to hand her a cupcake. "Everyone gets cupcakes today, no reason. And I'll give you a pass this time for turning in such an interesting article."

Lila didn't understand why this was happening, furious at being offered food. Especially something she'd want to eat so badly. And why did he tell her the article was interesting, even though he probably didn't read it? She imagined it was out of pity. She imagined his kindness was fake. Like she suspected, there were no honest people in this world.

She refused the cupcake and wouldn't look at his desk for the rest of the hour, nervous about her impulse control. On instinct, she gazed out of the classroom windows, despising this compulsion in herself that filled her with grave panic even though she couldn't stop doing it. The view overlooked a grass field, a flag pole, cars in the parking lot. She wondered if the insects liked to gaze at her through the window, too, as if she and her fellow students looked to them like ants in an ant farm, marching along to their classes, dutifully working, aimlessly circling the same glass walls, not realizing their overwhelming effort was just a pointless, repetitive march to their own demise. Toiling away for some hidden, all-knowing queen who wasn't there, who wouldn't save them, who would watch them slowly die behind that glass without mercy.

Seeing nothing outside, she moved her gaze to checking the walls. Focused on some black spot in the corner, she couldn't tell if it was an insect. It looked like it was maybe moving. She blinked, not sure if she could trust herself, not sure if she could trust to look away and risk losing wherever it went if it was real.

Then she felt a tickle at the back of her neck, something shifting past her braid. Something crawling in it. She flinched and reached at her braid right as the kid sitting behind her snatched something from her hair. When she felt this, she screamed in a gasp-jump and then buried her head in her hands in embarrassment.

She didn't see what, but he was hiding something in his lap. His face was red, fighting belly laughter with his friend sitting beside him also laughing, while Lila was trying not to unravel into hysterics.

"Lila, everything all right?" the substitute called out, not looking up from grading.

Lila nodded, mortified at this outburst, trying not to draw more attention to herself.

At her rescue, the bell rang for lunch, Lila's most dreaded time of the school day. She zipped up her bag and slung it over her shoulder, keeping her focus on reading her book while walking, a skill she had mastered.

The boys tormenting her followed her, then stepped in her way, blocking the path. The two of them were much bigger than her, and she didn't know a safe way around them. She hated that feeling with Marcus, too. How he used his towering presence as a constant threat. To remind her that at any moment he could pick her up, push her over, hold her down, do what he wanted.

One of them leaned forward, getting close to her face, still taking bites of his cupcake. Even though his breath made her want to gag, she wanted the cupcake. She wanted to shovel ten of them in her mouth and then vomit. She wanted to feel in control of something.

"Want some?" he asked her, holding it to her mouth.

Yes, she thought. She shook her head, and tried to ignore him, hoping not to rile any worse behavior from them, waiting for them to move so she could walk away.

"Forgot, this one only eats dick," he said and elbowed his friend who roared into laughter. He dug into his jeans pocket and cradled something in his hand.

Then he slapped her on the back, hard. He pulled at the open pouch in the front of her backpack and put whatever he was holding inside, zipping it closed for her.

"Got a little present for you, bug slut. One I think you'll *really* like." He laughed in unison with the echoed laughter of his friend as they finally brushed past her in the hallway.

Instantly, Lila tensed up. She remembered when Marcus would tell her to check her backpack for bugs, insisting that if she didn't check, she could never know what was in there. How the dark crevices of a backpack were a perfect hiding place, meaning he put something in there. She flashed back to earthworm dissection week in biology, how the whole time she had to hide from Marcus at school, knowing he would try to dispose of mangled worm corpses in the bottom of her bag.

Blinking away tears welling in her eyes, she tried to will them not to run down her face. She unzipped her backpack with trembling fingers. Inside the front pouch lurked a plastic glow-in-the-dark spider, its muted green light emanating from the blackness.

She wanted to go home, to sink into bed, to never have to face the world, her fate. It's not like Marcus would have helped her if he had been here. He would have laughed at her too.

She found the first open table in the cafeteria plaza to log this in her journal. The empty space across from her loomed, a void where Marcus would sit, the empty outline of his absence.

Opening her journal, she wrote: *Some asshole put a fake, glow-in-the-dark spider in my backpack. It made me cry.* She wanted to write further, but no words would come.

Glancing around, she watched kids shovel food into their mouths, uncaring if people watched them eat, or how much they ate, or what it was. Something Lila couldn't imagine, but burned with envy for. How free it would be to live like that. To just be normal.

Overwhelmed, not knowing what to write, she rested her head on the table.

"May I?" a voice asked.

When she looked up, she saw the substitute teacher from her last class standing there, whose name she couldn't recall. The one who had a reputation for being overly friendly and nice to the girls. The one most girls in her grade thought was hot. She thought he was weird, though. Everyone else just couldn't see through his appearance,

He sat across from her before she could answer. "Here," he offered up a half of the sandwich he brought, but she shook her head.

"You know I'm going to be teaching here full-time soon," he said, taking a bite and setting his water flask down.

I don't care, Lila thought, and could already feel the anxiety swelling in her throat with this conversation, though she didn't know why. It's not like he'd ever done anything to her. "Oh, cool," she said, not sure how to interact with teachers, especially this one. She didn't trust authority figures, or adults. Anyone, really.

"Yeah, World Literature! You know what I was thinking? You should be my TA. I wrote you in for third hour, with my AP Seniors. You're smarter than all of them anyway."

Lila didn't understand why he would say this. How could he know she was smarter if he didn't even know who his students were yet? Especially since he barely even knew her?

"So, when you fill out your class requests, you're guaranteed the spot. You'll grade papers, have the whole hour with me. We can do whatever, chill. I'll let you watch movies. I'll bring you Starbucks. Well, once you're…" he gestured to her stomach.

Lila wasn't sure, but she could almost detect the tiniest waft of alcohol on his breath, and glanced at the water bottle. It reminded her of her father.

"My classroom is just going to be one of the trailers behind the football field for now, until they build the new wing, but I start after winter break," he said, taking another bite, chewing for a moment in silence. "Seriously. Anything you want. You know I'm good for it," he said. As if this was something she could possibly know.

Lila didn't know what to say, so she said nothing.

"What kind of books do you like? I know you're a reader. You like Russian literature? That's what I'm focusing on for the semester."

He pulled a book out from his messenger bag and placed it on the table. It was one Lila had never heard of, *Roadside Picnic* by Arkady and Boris Strugatsky.

"You'll really like this book. Very intelligent. And I can't teach this one because it's banned too," he said, as if struggling to decide if he should bring it up. He rummaged through a separate pocket. "I'm sure you've read it anyway. Did you like *Lolita*? Classic Russian text. You like complex characters? Beautiful prose? Even better, *The Enchanter*. Nabokov's first attempt at this story. You can really see how he develops the concept. The way it haunted him for decades." He set *The Enchanter* beneath *Roadside Picnic*.

"I don't want to be a TA. I wouldn't be good at it," she said, trying to ease the sting of her rejection, hoping he wouldn't get angry.

"You'll change your mind," he assured.

No, I won't, she thought.

"I used to be like you. Doubting myself. Hiding in books. I know things are hard right now. It must be lonely. But you're not alone." He patted her hand in a way that she assumed was meant to be comforting, but it put her on edge.

Despite the fact that there was nothing egregiously wrong in this moment, she could feel it, his predatory brilliance. Marcus had given her speeches about this. The way predators can stalk out and smell prey, the most vulnerable. Marcus had it, too. That same brilliance.

"Thanks," she mumbled, unsure what else to do. Suddenly, she missed Marcus. She hated this, missing one terrifying male because he could protect her from other ones. "But no thank you, actually. It's okay," she said quietly, calmly pushing the books back over to him, not wanting to accept any kind of gifts for fear of owing something, or him thinking she was accepting the TA position. She realized she was being so mousy because she was afraid. This same tentativeness would emerge when she was with Marcus. This felt familiar.

"What do you mean, 'no'?" he laughed. "You love books. Just take them. I have more copies. I'm expecting you to help me lead discussions. You're such a smart girl. I don't think other girls your age can understand this book's material like you can," he said, not specifying which book he meant.

Other girls. Lila was so disgusted with hearing this. Like they were some pest population to be exterminated, but she was a single one who could be spared, so long as she was obedient, receptive, and separate from them—aka, isolated.

"And here, I've got one more for you."

Did he bring these to lunch just to give them to me? Lila thought, confused.

"It's not Russian, and it will be more of a horror book for you. But you'll appreciate it." He set *The Metamorphosis* on top of the stack.

"I already—" Lila tried to say, but at that moment, a buzzing roared past her ear, and a bee hovered over her sweatshirt, then landed on the ends of her hair. She tried not to scream, overtaken with fear. Her eyes widened, pleading for help. "Is it on me?" she whispered in a panic, trying not to move.

"Now," he said, "this isn't one of the ones from your article. Just a friendly bumblebee." He gently plucked it off of her and allowed it to walk along his fingers. Its movements appeared weak, slow, easy to kill if he felt like it. "See? Sweet as ever. Must be why it stopped. It likes how sweet you are," he said.

Lila felt nauseous, targeted.

"Why are you so afraid of them anyway?" He asked this with a smile, delighting in hearing about what scared her.

"Because. I think they're going to kill me."

He laughed and shook his head, as if she said something funny.

Finally, he ate the last bit of his sandwich, stood, and wiped at his mouth with a napkin. "Let me know what you think of those books," he reminded. He left them on the table, and she stared at them, afraid to take them, also afraid to leave them there.

Lila looked to her journal, wanting to log the bee, but for some reason, she was scared to write about what happened. Opening it again, she saw something scrawled near the bottom of the page.

Stupid slut.

Panic and shame welled inside her as she stared at the sloppy, nearly illegible writing.

Did someone take my journal? She started to freak out, wondering if those guys from class wrote in it, paranoid that someone may have read her entries, but the more she examined the writing, she couldn't deny its familiar slant and loops.

Is this… Is this my handwriting? Or…

Now she couldn't tell if she had written it, or if it was Marcus. A fear came over her that Marcus's spirit was watching her, communicating with her, panicking that her visions were somehow morphing into mediumship. He'd be fuming with jealousy that a male teacher spoke to her. Maybe he was reminding her that this was her fault. Everything was always her fault.

I don't know how to make them all go away, she scrawled back to him. *Help me.*

Lila's eyes filled with tears again. Feeling defeated, she buried her head in her hands. She wanted to binge something. Lila thought about chasing down that teacher and asking him for the rest of the cupcakes, ditching her next class, then hiding in the bathroom all period to throw up. Before she could go through with it, the bell rang again.

She groaned, picking up her backpack. Glancing to the journal beneath what she wrote, the lines were blank. Marcus didn't write back. He didn't need to. She knew exactly what he thought of her, the ways he'd punish her if he had the chance. She couldn't escape the feeling that everything terrible in her life was something she had earned, and that soon, it was only going to get worse.

VI

LILA COULDN'T WAIT for this appointment, to share what happened. Without Marcus to talk to anymore, she was looking forward to recounting every bug she saw that week to Dr. Peralta. She spoke at length about the bee that landed in her hair, then about the article she'd turned in, omitting everything that happened with her teacher, and when she got to the journal entry about the glow-in-the-dark spider in her backpack, Dr. Peralta interjected.

"Wait—how long have you been getting bullied?"

"I'm not getting bullied. I mean, I don't care. They're idiots. They don't matter."

"You wrote that it made you cry. That sounds like it matters to me. You're diminishing what happened to you, and your feelings about it."

"No, I mean, in the grand perspective of everything. The return is coming. Plus, it's nothing compared to what Marcus would do. It's why those guys at school even did it. They'd seen Marcus put bugs in my backpack before. It was a joke." Lila made air quotes for the word *joke.* "Anyway, about the bee—they're almost here. The waiting is torture, not knowing the exact moment of the return," Lila said,

"Lila…" Dr. Peralta shook her head. "Insects have been here long before us, and I hate to tell you this because I know this will be disturbing to you, but they will be here long after. They will survive us all."

Lila cringed. She thought of radioactive cockroaches, of mutant flying insects with strange venomous growths and contaminated particles speckled all over their thoraxes, of a human wasteland lost to nuclear war. Of insects and detritivores skittering out of the rubble, freeing themselves from the dark confines of the sewers, scrabbling above ground to feast on a sea of billions of corpses, on the remnants of whatever animals or organic matter remained in an aftermath of humanity's own undoing.

She felt panicky, her palms sweating, her adrenals out of control from the years of bulimia and the constant, exhaustive labor of having parasitic life inside her.

"Maybe we can work on some acceptance strategies?" Dr. Peralta asked. "Of coping with this as a concrete fact, finding a way to learn to live alongside the insects. To make peace with this as an example of something in life that we cannot control."

Lila nearly guffawed into laughter—in disbelief at the stupid things people said, anything to discredit the obvious, to not have to look at what was coming.

"That's not going to happen. All I think about are insects."

"And when you have these invasive thoughts, what fears come to you? For example, you might feel you are not safe. I hear so much about these bugs, but I don't hear enough about you. About your inner world. How you really feel."

"Same stuff I've been saying. The insects are my inner world. They're my entire life."

"Seems to me, it's the opposite—that they block out your inner world."

"Marcus was fine with me talking about the return. I
don't understand why everyone else acts like it's a crime."

Dr. Peralta paused. "Why don't you tell me about the
last time you saw him?"

Lila's mind flooded with images, the memory of the
cabin suffocating her like a heavy fog, bits of it lost to
blackouts of the chaos. She went over the narrative she'd
said a thousand times already.

"It was an awful night. I don't remember all of it. Marcus
said he wanted to do something special for me, take me on
a different type of date, something we'd never done before.

"He drove us up to Mt. Hawk. We went to this ca—place,"
she caught herself. She almost said cabin. "This creepy place.
In the middle of nowhere, by some campground area, even
though I said I didn't want to go camping. That, obviously,
camping was going to be difficult for me." Lila said this
with a clear frustration in her voice. "That it's outside, I'd
be in a panic the whole time. I could hear the murmuring
of insects, them whirring around everywhere. I refused to
get out of the car."

"I imagine he didn't take that well," Dr. Peralta said,
picking a spot of lint off of her blazer and grabbing her
notes.

Lila remembered the look on Marcus's face when she
had tried to refuse, the instant escalation of his anger.

"GET OUT, LILA. Get out of the car."

"I said I don't want to. I already told you I don't want
to camp or hike, okay? It's dark, please don't make me.
Let's just leave. Please, can we just go?"

"Lila, it's them or us. You can't keep living like this. It's pathetic. Now get out." He gripped her arm and pulled her with all his force, releasing her carelessly, the harsh whiplash of the movement almost making her fall over. He closed the car door and clicked the lock button on the key fob, two beeps confirming she wouldn't be able to get back in to the safety of walls protecting her from outside. From the insects. "It's not that far. You'll like where we're going, you'll see. Or just stand there if you want, but I'm not unlocking it."

Lila started to walk, hoping that wherever he was taking her would have some kind of shelter. She crossed her arms tightly against herself, paying close attention to any noises, if anything was flying close to her. When they trudged uphill to an even more desolate area, the outline of a cabin emerged from behind some trees. She was instantly suspicious, wondering how Marcus knew about this area. "Whose cabin is this? Are you sure it's okay for us to be here?"

He didn't answer her, leaving Lila to believe that he didn't know whose it was either, that he wasn't invited. When she realized he didn't have a key, and that he was breaking in, her feet turned to lead. He wriggled open the window.

"Come on," he waved his hand and motioned to her, wanting her to climb through. "Look, no webs," he said and shined his phone, the glow emanating around the windowpane.

"I think we should go, Marcus. We could get in trouble."

"No one is even here! You can't get in trouble for shit no one knows about. You freak out about everything! It's constant drama with you. In ten seconds, I'm going to close and lock this window. You can stay outside. Good luck if the return comes tonight."

Lila scanned her surroundings, searching for if there was anywhere else to go, or anything she could do, but there wasn't. She couldn't see much because of the dim moonlight, only endless trees and rough terrain, realizing that even if she did hike back to the car, even if she broke the window to get in, the swarms could fly in too. Then it would be a disaster dealing with Marcus. Even if she stole the keys and ran, he would catch up to her, overpower her. And then he'd be so mad, she couldn't imagine what he would do.

So, she came forward, and he lifted her up, helping her through the window.

Inside, she was immediately taken with the stillness of the room. The quilted blankets thrown over the couch. The quaint, cozy feel. How peaceful the cabin might be in a different context, somewhere to read for days and get lost to the world.

That feeling abruptly left her once she noticed around twenty animal heads or more lining the walls. The taxidermized heads unnerved her, the way they were staring down at her. A premonitory blackness glinted in their glass eyes, a knowing. There was a crossbow and a few rifles mounted on the wall, a fog of death everywhere.

"See, baby, how upset you got about nothing? Look how beautiful it is in here." Marcus walked over to the fireplace, grabbing his lighter and igniting the pile of wood, poking at it with the fire poker. "Almost as beautiful as you." He smiled like he wanted something. "I knew you'd love it."

She hadn't told him she loved it here. She hadn't told him anything.

He leaned over and kissed her. She'd stayed frozen and lifeless, like her volume was turned way down, her movements slowed, her brain muted.

He grabbed her hand and pulled her close to him in a tight embrace that felt more like being contained or held captive than anything resembling a hug. Marcus had never been affectionate, this was not his usual behavior.

"Come here," he said. "Get by the fire with me." He lay down on the knitted rug in front of the fireplace and pretended to stare into it for a moment, waiting for her. He barely made it two seconds before his gaze fell to her body.

She listened, reluctantly.

"Get close, it's cold." he said as she lay down and he pulled her to him, rubbing up against her ass. "See how nice it is for us to be together like this? It's quiet here. Let me warm you up." He kissed her neck and her spine prickled in revulsion.

Quiet. As in, no one is around, Lila thought. *Scream and no one will hear you.*

Refusing him would get nowhere. At best, one of his yelling fits. At worst, one of his tests that involved her being locked outside all night. Maybe he'd tell on her, say she broke into this place. Maybe something really bad would happen.

She didn't say anything, didn't return any affection, didn't argue, didn't revolt. She just lay there, mentally bracing for whatever he was about to do.

Marcus stuck his hand up her shirt, then impatiently started working on getting his pants down. And soon after, hers. He whispered in her ear, "Come on, baby. Don't be so tense." He moved her onto her back, then spit into his hand and stroked himself. He got on top of her.

Lila didn't do anything, let her thoughts turn to static. For a minute, she even tried to convince herself that this was a good thing, that it would make Marcus happy. That happy Marcus would mean calm Marcus. That maybe he'd be a lot nicer now. That this would be worth it.

She didn't look at him, didn't think about what was happening, ignoring the pain as he pushed into her, how much worse it got with his vigorous motions, trying to suffer through the heat from the fire being too close and the sweat already collecting at his hairline, flinching when a droplet of it pattered against her eyebrow. And him saying, "Relax," when she unconsciously stiffened, then him trying to open her legs wider whenever she'd tighten up, and she lay there looking past his head to the hunted heads on the walls, the taxidermized animals all around her. She had felt a strange kinship with them, forever at the mercy of men who take a body in conquest. Who will hang your decapitated head as a prize.

When Marcus gripped her tightly pressing all his weight on her, and finally stopped moving, she exhaled, maybe for the first time that entire time. Her heartbeat thrummed in her ears, the only sound layering over the silence, the crackling fire, and Marcus's slightly out-of-breath panting. He tapped her stomach, petting her like a dog, in some gesture of recognition, wordless acknowledgment. But he didn't kiss her, didn't call her baby anymore, didn't speak.

Once he grabbed his pants to put them back on, she pulled a blanket over herself and dressed with her back turned to him. Each motion robotic. Too dazed to even cry. She stayed silent. He sat looking into the flames for a moment, a smirk on his face. This is when she knew she had left herself back there, in the locked car, and the body that walked her into this cabin wasn't fully under the control of her brain.

Two moths had flown into the fireplace, and Lila stared at them, watching them kill themselves in the flames. She thought maybe they were a couple in love, chasing after the light. In this moment she realized she never should have told Marcus about the return, that people will take any vulnerability and use it to hurt you.

Another moth followed the first two, and Marcus snatched it mid-flight.

Lila gasped, the action startling her out of her momentary trance.

"Here, let me help you with that," he said, gripping the moth by its wings, chalky residue gathering on his fingers already. The moth was twitching, trying to escape.

"Stop it," she said softly, but with intention. She was good at sticking up for others, just never herself. "Let it go."

"Now why would I do that?" he said as he flicked his lighter and brought the flame up to it.

"Stop!" Lila screamed.

"I'm just helping it out. This is what the damn thing wants anyway, flames." He started to burn it, its legs wiggling in desperation before he singed its body entirely and then abruptly let it go, resulting in a few miserable moments of its engulfed wings flapping frantically before it dropped blackened to the floor. He stomped on it and kicked the last chalky bit of its corpse to the side and dusted his hands off on his jeans.

Lila started to cry. "What is wrong with you?" she said, more as a statement than a question, wracked with sudden distress at processing everything that had just happened.

"I protected you," he said, putting an unlit cigarette into his mouth. "Gave that moth exactly what it wanted. It was going to die anyway. What's the difference?"

In a daze, Lila wiped her eyes and stood up, suddenly making a decision before she could think about it. She quickly reached for the keys Marcus had left on the counter.

"I wouldn't do that," Marcus said calmly, and she held them in a frozen pause before setting them back down. Processing, she turned and ran toward the window.

"I definitely wouldn't do that," he added, more threatening this time.

She tried to ignore him, but it didn't matter. He followed her, let her struggle with the window latch for a second, then grabbed her and picked her up like she was nothing more than the moth he just thoughtlessly lit on fire. He set her back down on the rug by the fireplace.

"Stop being such a bitch," he hissed at her, and his eyes shifted into the dead eyes he'd get when anger overtook him. "It's always something with you! Just sit down. I'm going to smoke. Don't you fucking dare get up, and don't make me come back in here. We'll leave in a second, when I say so," he said and glared at her. He was still clutching her arm so tightly that it was going numb, then he turned nonchalantly to head out to the deck.

Lila's eyes glazed over, defeated by her failed escape, looking back into the fire. Her limbs felt momentarily useless, her body heavy. She realized she understood why they do that, the moths. Why they want so desperately for something to set them free. This idea entranced her, these creatures of the night longing for emancipation from their darkness. She reached a hand out to the flame, considering this. Trying to warm herself, even though her heart was racing and she was sweaty with adrenaline. She thought about extending her hand all the way in, just to see how it would feel, something to take her mind off of the fear.

Then blackness started dotting along her vision, a buzzing pain amplifying her senses, her instincts. Something like survival came to the surface. Lila's eyes drifted across the room, feeling more of a pull of impulse than a conscious decision to move. She looked to the fire poker, picked it up, and followed Marcus outside.

"Lila? Lila? Did you hear me? Seems I lost you there for a second. Are you all right?"

"YEAH," LILA SAID and blinked a few times, rousing herself to the present moment.

"I was saying I imagine he didn't take that well? What did he do? When you refused to get out of the car? Dr. Peralta asked again.

It took Lila a minute to craft her answer, deciding how to tell Dr. Peralta about what Marcus did, and had to come up with a sugarcoated version. She hadn't told this detail to anyone else. Not like she had to with the pregnancy. But no one knew that this was the only night. *The* night. The conception.

"He took it better than I thought, I guess, said we could get in the backseat and talk. But Marcus just really wanted to have sex. We still hadn't, and he was getting so impatient. He kept grabbing at me, whispering in my ear. I knew he wasn't going to stop, so I just let it happen."

Dr. Peralta visibly recoiled at this statement and wrote something down.

"After it was over, there was this noise. Something outside, like a low growl. He was certain it was a bear, which made no sense, but said he wanted to see. He took the keys and locked the doors, told me to stay in the car no matter what. I begged him to let us leave, drive home. But it was Marcus. He never listened." Lila paused. "It's weird, I can't remember some of the details from that night, like it goes black in parts," she said.

"That can happen with traumatic incidents. We may have a dissociation response. Maybe more of it will come back to you that spurs your memory. Right now, don't blame yourself if it feels blurry."

I wish it was even blurrier, Lila thought. But Lila did remember how she made sure to get the cigarette, how she had to find the butt later to remove the evidence. How she stood behind him and squared her shoulders like she was about to swing a home run, hit him over the head with that fire poker, the metal making loud contact with his skull. The way he crumpled over like a rag doll, a spot of blood trickling out from his wound and running down his neck, leaving a red trail when she dragged him, lugging his dead weight with all her might and managing to lay him into the belly of the tub. She remembered the bloody clothes burning in the fireplace, how she spent three hours scrubbing out the stains of her sins with hydrogen peroxide and bleach from the cabinet.

"It's hard to talk about this," Lila could feel herself getting emotional. "I waited thirty minutes before I tried to call him. My service was awful, the calls weren't even going through. I was scared that if I called sooner, the bear or whatever would hear his phone ring." *It took me thirty minutes to drag him inside. Then I had to deal with the blood that the gash on his head smeared from the deck to the carpet to the bathroom tile.*

"I worried that maybe the bear got him after all, that he was in danger." *I wanted to be free, drown him in the tub, dump him in the lake.*

"After repeatedly trying to call him, I forced myself to get out and look. 'Be brave,' I could hear his voice telling me." *I looked at his unconscious face, his nostrils flaring with each heavy breath, the trickle of red by his eye. Then I looked at the drain in the tub. Be brave, I told myself.*

"This is where it gets really foggy. All I remember next is running. I fell down a ridge, thought I broke my ankle. I'm not sure if I passed out or what. Next thing I know some forest ranger is dragging me out, and EMS is questioning me, asking if I'm alone, trying to figure out what happened to me. I told them Marcus and I got separated, that something bad was out there. A bear. Some animal. How Marcus went searching for whatever it was, that they had to find him. As I was telling them, the mosquitoes were whining, gathering around my legs, ravenous for my scraped-up bloody knees. It's been about eight months now," she gestured at her belly, "that he's been missing. At this point, everyone thinks he's dead. Search and Rescue said the first twenty-four hours are crucial with missing persons. All they found were his phone and car keys at the bottom of the lake." *The lake where I threw them.*

"I… I…" Lila started to choke up. "I don't want to think about this anymore. I don't want to talk about this," she said.

Dr. Peralta had an empathetic expression on her face. "I'm so sorry, Lila. I had no idea. Your mother only told me that you lost him, but I assumed she meant he was deceased. This is all incredibly traumatic."

Then she sat for a moment, blinking in silence, processing. "So, what I'm hearing is, he took you to a remote location that you did not want to go to in order to coerce you into having sex. Then he decided to go after some supposed threat outside, took the keys, and left you there alone? Weaponizing your phobia, knowing you would be too afraid to leave the car? Lila, did he ever give you any indication that he wanted to hurt you?"

Lila flashed to tons of instances of his cruelty, his tests, all the horrible things he'd say. "I don't know. I mean, he was my only friend."

Dr. Peralta shook her head. "I understand you're grieving. Maybe you blame yourself."

Lila's eye twitched a little at hearing this, and she hoped it wasn't noticeable.

"And the vulnerability you're feeling, carrying his baby. I acknowledge the events of his disappearance are difficult, but I believe this story may have ended differently, in you not sitting across from me right now. Maybe after some distance from these experiences, you'll realize you survived. That, sometimes, our losses save us."

"Maybe," Lila said softly, unsure how to react organically, inconspicuously.

"I know all of this is overwhelming. Are you feeling present? That was a lot. For right now, I want to make sure you're taking care of yourself. Have you been eating?"

Lila struggled to stifle her annoyance at this question. "I mean, I try to."

Dr. Peralta paused and folded her hands together on her lap. "Lila, do you happen to know what the deadliest mental health disorder is? It surprises people. Do you know what it is?"

Lila shook her head.

"Eating disorders. Specifically, anorexia nervosa. I'm concerned about you. If you are suffering with an eating disorder, it's not only detrimental to your health, but it may cause birth defects or be fatal to your baby. I think that—"

"I don't have an eating disorder," Lila lied, bleary-eyed with hunger, stomach growling. Nervously, she stuffed her hands inside her pockets and stammered on before Dr. Peralta had any time to protest the interruption. "It's just the bugs. Really. If I had an eating disorder, I would be thin, and I'm not. I'm average. I have a huge belly. Don't you see this?" Lila gestured to her pregnant stomach. "I've seen pregnant girls with disordered eating, and you can't even tell they're five, six months along. That's *clearly* not me."

"You wouldn't lie to me, Lila, would you?" Dr. Peralta asked, a detective look in her eyes. "Not everyone with an eating disorder is thin, and I think you know that."

Lila had to flip this around. She raised her voice at Dr. Peralta. "Everyone blames what I'm saying on anything else—disorders, phobias, hormones. Acting like I'm crazy! It's wrong, the way everyone treats me. And they do it because I tell them what they don't want to hear, what they refuse to acknowledge. I know I'll never be able to make you believe me. You just want to pawn me off or blame what I say on whatever diagnosis you come up with, to ignore me like everyone else."

Dr. Peralta did not bend at this. "Lila, when did you start hating your body?"

"I don't hate my body! I just wish everyone would leave me alone about it!" Lila yelled.

"Who's everyone? Hating your body is not uncommon during pregnancy, or during puberty for that matter."

"I don't know, you. My mom. Marcus. Boys at school always staring at me, saying stupid things, trying to rip things from my hands to get me to look at them, snap my bra straps, grab me, push me, pick me up. My teachers. Old men gawking at me with their wives right next to them. It feels like everyone is looking at me all the time. I don't know how to make it stop."

Dr. Peralta continued to write a few notes.

"So, you're feeling objectified and vulnerable?"

"I don't know. I just…" Lila sighed. "I wish I looked different. That I *was* different. Someone no one ever noticed. That I could be a ghost. Be the kind of invisible that means I don't even exist. That I'd be never leered at, never made fun of."

"They're probably making fun of you because they like you," she said.

"No. None of them like me. No one likes me. I see the girls they like. They're playful how they tease them, and they dote on them. They laugh together, try to impress them. That's not what they do to me. They treat me like they want to hurt me. The things they do to me… It's meant with cruelty." Lila's eyes welled up and she turned her head away to hide her tears. "I thought Marcus liked me, but even he didn't. He just wanted to hurt me too."

"What do you mean by that?"

"Exactly what I said. He didn't like me. I didn't matter to him at all."

"No, the part about wanting to hurt you." Dr. Peralta said this with a knowing look, waiting for Lila to connect it.

Lila shrugged. "He just…" As Lila said this, she could see a morphing reflection of his face taking over hers in the glass in Dr. Peralta's coffee table. Lila looked away from it, not wanting to see his eyes glaring at her. A shudder of fear traveled through her jaw, and she realized she was grinding her teeth. She tried to relax.

"I just mean… I guess you're right. He probably did want to hurt me. Worse even, I think, than the ways he tried to hurt everyone else."

VII

NAZARET TURNED THE key to lock her office door, getting ready to leave for the day, when her psychiatrist colleague from down the hall walked past.

"Hey, Nazaret, how are you? I hope you don't mind me saying, I've been meaning to check on you. You look tired lately. Hope everything is okay."

"I'm not sleeping well. Lots of stress with my caseload. It's been a weird few weeks."

"Maybe you should take a break and come with me to that seminar next month? I can't wait to get out of my house. We randomly got bedbugs. Can you believe that? They're so disgusting, it's been hell getting rid of them. Makes me miss the DDT days," she cackled. "So what if it's a carcinogen, everything's a carcinogen these days. Might make a few kids deformed, but at least it doesn't take weeks to clean out an infestation!" She laughed some more as if this was hilarious. Nazaret found this comment especially disturbing coming from a health professional, but tried not to judge, hoping it was an awkward throwaway remark and not a reflection of character.

"I've never dealt with bedbugs, sorry you're going through that," Nazaret offered. "Your earrings are interesting, by the way," she added, trying to change the subject, not admitting that they grossed her out, those oversized heart-shaped earrings containing dead bugs.

"I got them at the jewelry expo! They're real ladybugs in amber! Not even imitation. Aren't they just darling?" She clutched at her left ear, palming the earring and tilting it forward so that Nazaret could get a closer look.

Nazaret examined the murky hearts with fossilized insects. The dead ladybugs weren't big enough to be sure, but Nazaret could almost see an anguish cast over their miniscule faces, longing to be freed from this prison—suspended in heart shaped amber tombs. Forced to hang from the flesh of a woman on a bug killing spree. As if their corpses were heads on a stake for some war-crazed king, a warning to the bedbugs, or maybe the other way around. A call to action. A target dangling from both ears: this human equals enemy. And the ladybugs, doomed for all time to occupy this territory, screeching battle cries for vengeance, forever waving their red shells in amber like flags of their dead.

"Well I'm glad I bumped into you. I've been wanting to tell you that soon I'll be going on leave." She smiled wide, pausing for effect. "Because I'm pregnant! With twins! I'm so excited, but I want to keep it hush-hush until I make the announcement."

"Congratulations! That's wonderful," Nazaret said. She immediately thought of these twins suffering complications from DDT exposure, prematurely dying in utero, or being born without limbs, then thought of when she was thirty-four and in a panic, almost froze her eggs before she got pregnant only six months later.

That same unease came back to her now. *My eggs,* she thought. "I'm thinking about having another one," she said,

"Is that right? I vote you should," the psychiatrist said, her ladybug amber earrings sagging down her stretched earlobes, too heavy for her ears.

"Don't infect me," Nazaret said. "Baby fever is a disease. You know how it is, once somebody in here gets pregnant, then the whole fucking building is suddenly with child."

ON THE DRIVE home, the rain spit violently onto the road. The windshield wipers were barely helping, and the headlights illuminated just enough to see a few feet ahead. Despite the mist of sheeted water and fog, Nazaret's thoughts drifted to Gabe. She didn't know what to do with herself, all this chaos fluttering through her mind, the emptiness she refused to acknowledge, this sudden urgency about her eggs.

She called him and put him on speaker, let the phone cradle on her knees. "Hi! I'm coming home right now. Is it raining there? It's pouring over here! The kids are still with your sister, right?"

"Sorry, I can't really hear you," he said, his slight lisp coming through. She always found it endearing. "Hang on, let me close the window."

She heard Gabe walk over to the window, him rustling around trying to close it.

"They are loud, aren't they?" he said, "The cicadas. Mating season."

Nazaret twitched a little at that word, it suddenly made her feel hot. *Mating.* It's what she wanted. Needed, even. To mate. Then she felt a sting of heartbreak, rage. Even though she tried to shove it down, this wound had been festering over the years. All the times she tried to compete with random women, to get his attention again, always failing. Her desire constantly self-restrained.

She had been wanting to fuck constantly lately, the way those creatures do, something carnal and unrelenting, something weird. She was too forgiving with Gabe's mediocrity, his infidelities, because she always believed love is bigger than the physical realm, but now she was unsure. Now she wanted to experience some great sexual legacy, something to rival the way those insects fucked on even in the face of death. She loved that in some insect species, females would devour their male, all part of their natural order. The way they knew, those simple males, that they had a singular life purpose: to please and then die.

She delighted in this. She thought again of nurturing young. How long had it been since her children were born? How long had it been since she'd been fucked like she was meant for something other than his pleasure?

Anger flashed through her, a surfacing truth that she didn't even want him. Maybe it was a hint of vengeance blooming, but she wanted to abandon purity and love. She wanted to feel wrong. Powerful. To awaken something. Amass an army. To see tons of little mouths at her command, ready to overthrow the world, calling after her: *mother.*

For a moment, she recalled the horror of almost dying in childbirth with her youngest during her C-section, the surgeon sluicing her open and seeing blood everywhere like some B horror movie, him digging inside of her, slipping past her organs with his gloved hands while he was pulling her son's purpling face out from her belly, the entire medical team rushing to get that umbilical cord off of his neck. Recalling perfectly the torture of barely being able to move for weeks, recovering from the most traumatic physical experience of her life. An experience she inexplicably wanted to risk again.

It occurred to her now that Gabe had always been so boring. The only thing interesting about him was the constant threat of losing him. She had given her loyalty, endured betrayal, for what? If he could do whatever he wanted, she could, too. Maybe another could give her what she needed. Maybe another could fertilize her eggs. Maybe Dr. Jones from the third floor, with his dimpled smile and long eyelashes. Or maybe tall Dr. Gutierrez could make her beautiful, big children. Or even that new intern who liked her, who was a decade younger and dumber than dirt, but a perfect physical specimen. An ideal mate. Likely had a sperm count these older men couldn't compete with. Maybe he could match her intensity lingering under the surface that she needed mirrored back, even once. She didn't want to have to hide anymore, the part of her Gabe always tried to dull and snuff out.

"Sorry, okay, I'm back," he said.

"Can we talk when I get home?"

"About what?" his tone shifted, immediately irritated.

"Nothing, never mind. I'll be there soon." She pressed end on the call, resigning to her usual repression.

As she hung up, she saw something in the fog. A figure. Some ghostly form of dissipating mist. She squinted at it through her mirrors, trying to decipher what she saw, how it felt intimately familiar to her somehow. She couldn't imagine who it could have been, if it was her tata, herself, or something else? While she was looking in the rearview, a splatter of massacred wings hit the windshield and she shrieked, flinching at the sudden, small impact. *What did I hit?*

It was hard to tell in the dark, in the rain. A dense cloud of insect corpses littered the windshield, their broken wings like confetti across the glass. Were these moths? Or butterflies? A cloud of them flying to Mexico for their annual migration? Who were these dead souls she had just slaughtered? The wipers were smearing them around, and the rain began to quickly wash them away, though the evidence still remained. An unnerving rattle settled inside Nazaret. Something indescribable. Something like doom.

When she walked into the house, all hope for talking vanished. The growing, unrelenting darkness inside of her was overtaken by her appetite. The thrill of opportunity possessed her. She pushed Gabe onto the couch and crawled into his lap. "I missed you today," she lied, as she straddled him and started kissing his neck.

"Woah, hi. I missed you too," he tried to say before she put her lips on his. They started making out, and he was already getting hard. She unbuttoned his shorts and pulled his zipper down, and started to stick a hand through the slit of his boxer briefs. He shifted and pulled her closer, but she gasped and jerked her hand away.

"What?" He leaned forward, opened his eyes. "What's wrong?"

"Sorry, I thought I felt something move across my wrist. Like a bug." She examined her hand, finding nothing. Her hair was dangling over her shoulder, bunched up around her neck. "I guess it must have been my hair. It's getting so long."

He gathered her hair and held it for her, pawing at her shirt with his other hand and trying to take it off. She kissed him again and pulled his waistband down.

She slid to the edge of the couch and got onto her knees, then started licking him, teasing, worshiping him with a religious devotion.

His breath hitched in a sharp inhale. "Don't stop," he told her, and she could feel the thrum of blood coursing through him, his eagerness. She reveled in the anticipation of getting to taste him, the saltiness of his semen. Salt she wanted to drink. Something to fill her.

She kissed along his thighs, letting her teeth catch his skin, enjoying the feel of him. She was liking this much more than usual, this boundless, newfound sensuality. That of course he got to benefit from. But he was just the meat in front of her, what was available. She took little bites of him, wanting to feel the weight of him between her teeth, and she bit harder into his flesh. He flinched a little but didn't complain, and she bit him some more before letting her tongue move along the smorgasbord of his body, savoring the taste. Throughout this, desire fueled her, something unspeakable taking over, a yearning to sink her mouthparts in and feast. She had to force herself to pull back with the teeth, and licked him for maybe a full minute, whatever kept them both distracted, staying in control of these dark thoughts. Then she eased him down into the back of her throat.

With his dick sliding past her tonsils, she could feel the blaring sensation of that hunger buzz, that overwhelming feeling of wanting to bite, to chew, to clamp down on him with all her might. To just unhinge her jaw and bite his dick clean through in one voracious snap and swallow it down whole.

Fighting this, fearing herself, she pulled away once more, despite his small exhale of protest, and was about to crawl on top of him to fuck him when she felt something move across her wrist again.

"Fuck!" she shrieked.

They both looked to the moth fluttering up right between them, flying toward the ceiling light in the kitchen. She glanced behind Gabe, catching a glimpse of the sliding glass door. "Oh Jesus fucking Christ!" she said and buried her face into his knee.

A horde of moths were gathering at the windows. One moth the size of a hand was spread across the glass, and the smaller ones were fluttering all over, piling on top of each other in a frenzy, throwing themselves against the door in full force, wanting the light. To come in.

VIII

LILA WOKE IN a panicked daze, still momentarily lost in fear. She had been dreaming of Marcus again, suffering recurring nightmares of him lately. The only thing worse than the insect visions was seeing Marcus in her sleep.

It always started the same, some reiteration of the last time he came over after school. She was lying beside him, reading, and because he got jealous whenever she wasn't focused on him, he kept interrupting her.

"Are you a predator or are you prey?"

"I—"

"Answer me."

She set her textbook down, contemplating. "Neither, I guess. I would never want to hurt anyone."

"Wrong answer. It's one or the other, Lila. Say you're lying in bed, just like now, and you feel movement. It's the tiniest sensation, that feeling you get when you know one is close."

He pulled her shirt up a couple inches and put his hand below her belly button, pausing for a second, making her wait. "You look down and see a scorpion crawling across your stomach. What do you do?"

Lila just shook her head, the thought too disturbing to her.

"Do you know how to kill a scorpion? They're tough to kill, nearly invincible," he said matter-of-factly. "They withstand almost anything. Poisons rarely work. It can't penetrate them. They're too tough."

Lila said nothing, just listened.

"You can't freeze them. They hibernate. Yes they dominate hot climates, but they absorb the cold like it's nothing. If you flush them down the toilet, they'll endure just to spite you. They can live underwater for days. Starve it? They survive. No water for weeks? They survive. Their exoskeletons are difficult to crush. If you try to smash one on carpet, it might live. They flatten themselves to the thinness of a credit card, sneak through the tiniest crevices. They're masterful escape artists. They crawl on any surface besides smooth glass or something slick. Even upside down and across the ceiling, they rain down and fall on you in your sleep. Beds are one of their favorite shelters—you know this. They love to crawl up bedposts."

Lila's bed frame had glass jars under all four posts for this very reason.

"But you know what they can't live through? Being pierced. These violent creatures, you have to give them a fight. Beat them at their own game. Sure you could stomp on it if you've got shoes on. But if not? If this happens?" He dug his fingers into her skin. "Here's what you do. You slowly turn to your nightstand and grab this pen right here," he said as he snatched one off the top of her notebooks. "After it crawls off of you, take it and stab the damn thing through its fucking middle. Don't strike until you're certain it's the right moment. The hard part is doing this without getting stung or catching the pincers. It'll want to fight. An intimate death for an intimate creature. Stab it back. Fucking impale it. So, what are you going to do, Lila?" He crawled his hand up her torso with each finger slowly moving across her stomach. His pointer finger raised high, imitating a stinger. "Well?" he asked again, growing impatient. "What are you going to do?" His hand crept further.

"I don't know what I'd do," she said after a delay. "I'd just panic. I'd be frozen in fear."

He gripped her face with his other hand and turned her head to his. "No," he responded. "You'd think. You'd calculate, make a decision. You either let it sting you, or you sting it. You'd be brave. You'd stay calm, just watch. Don't react too quickly. Study it. Don't spook it and don't panic. Don't let it know what you're going to do. It's like with people, Lila. Your element of surprise is important. Never reveal your position. Don't let them know what you know. Don't flash your upper hand, just use it. It won't attack unless threatened, so don't let it know you're a threat. If you piss it off, it's over. It could sting you a million times then vanish through a slit in the wall and come back for vengeance the second you've forgotten it." He crawled his hand up to the very base of her ribs. Her second rib. "Now tell me, what will you do?"

"Marcus," Lila sighed, getting frustrated. "Stop. I already told you, I don't know."

"Wrong answer," he said and then jabbed his pointer finger into her side with a sudden force that made her gasp. "What the fuck are you going to do?" he asked more aggressively, and jabbed at her again, then a third time. He lowered his voice to a whisper, as if he wasn't sure he wanted to tell her this part. He pressed his mouth to her ear. "You think you're small and powerless, but you're not. The opposite is true. The smaller the scorpion, the deadlier."

"Stop it!" she yelled. "I don't know, okay? I'd try to push it away, wait for it to leave. I always have a blanket over me to protect me, so I'd kick the blanket off," she reasoned, knowing it was a ridiculous answer. Thinking about this made her spiral, realizing the ways she was not yet prepared to face her greatest fears.

"That's not how this goes, and you know it. It's under the blanket, Lila. What if it refuses to crawl off of you? What if it won't leave you alone? What if it crawls higher?" he said and shoved his hand under her bra.

Lila winced.

"Or what if it wants to crawl in your mouth?" he said and hooked his fingers against her bottom teeth, pulling her lips to his.

"Marcus—" she mumbled and turned her face away, trying not to unconsciously bite him at the shock of this. His fingers tasted like tobacco.

"Listen to me," he said, more as a command, but when he opened his mouth, Lila noticed something move across his tongue. When she could process what she was seeing, she realized it was a scorpion.

Frozen in terror, she could no longer hear what he was saying. She watched as it crawled past his lips and up the side of his cheek to his hairline, resting there, stinger poised, waiting for her. Marcus kept talking, suddenly furious that she was ignoring him, so he sat up and started yelling at her, but no sound came out. Before Lila could blink, tons of scorpions started spilling out of his mouth, then his jaw extended open wider, too wide, unhinging like a serpent, about to snap over her entire body and consume her. Upon his transformation, the arachnids skittered away in fear, save for one, who dutifully crawled toward Lila and waited at the center of her stomach. It sat there, watching her, wanting to make sure it held her gaze when it stung.

That was when Lila jolted awake in a startle. Heart racing, breath heavy. Her eyes darted around the bed, looking for subtle movement.

This Marcus dream was more disturbing than usual. She wondered if therapy was causing this, riling up her subconscious, making everything that had finally started to settle and bury become upturned and restless inside her.

She pulled the covers over her head to retreat under the blanket. In that moment, Lila could feel the tiniest movement of a scorpion falling from the ceiling and landing on her. She was sure of it. She gripped the pen she kept with her to sleep, white-knuckling it, ready to strike. But when she threw the covers back, all she saw was darkness.

IX

DRIZZLING RAIN PATTERED against the windows. Lila and Vivian sat together in the living room on opposite couches, Vivian watching some cooking show, Lila balancing a bug book inside of a baby book on her belly. Vivian got up to look out of the curtains, staring at the sky.

"Storm's coming," she said, peering out into the distance. "Look at those clouds. We're not supposed to see much of it until later in the week maybe, the forecast is all over the place. Apparently, we might get hail. One thing's for sure, something vicious is headed our way."

"I guess," Lila said dismissively.

"I thought you liked the rain. Bugs can't fly in the rain. That's good, right? You won't see them outside of your window."

Lila didn't respond, giving Vivian cold silence.

Vivian crossed her arms, returning back to the sky, lost in thought. "The night I found out I was pregnant with you, I hadn't even taken a test yet, and there was this dreadful storm. I was so afraid, and I'd never been afraid of storms before. Somehow, it hit me. I just knew.

I'm pregnant, I thought. And right in that instant, the world became a different place, a dangerous place. Even a rainstorm scared me. Everything a constant threat. I had to be afraid for all this world could do to you. All that I could not shield you from, the way control or certainty evaporated in that realization. I can't explain it, I knew you were going to be unique, my perfect creation. In the image of God, with his divine knowing. In my mind, I could see you, cradled in my arms—the future—the entire world in your eyes, all of its beauty, its terror. I was wracked with it my whole pregnancy, and it was such a stormy summer, too. You were finicky, even in the womb. I knew you were afraid of the storms. So, I'd sing to you."

Vivian started humming, then sang in her sweetest lullaby voice.

> *"The itsy bitsy spider climbed up the water spout,*
> *Down came the rain, and washed the spider out,*
> *Out came the sun, and dried up all the rain,*
> *And the itsy bitsy spider went—"*

"Ugh, Mom! Stop it!" Lila slapped her hands over her ears, disturbed by the thought of her mother tormenting her with songs about spiders even in utero, when she was defenseless and trapped, forced to listen because there was no escape. The sound of that song grating in her ears was already getting stuck in her head, even worse than the incessant buzzing.

Vivian scowled. "I wasn't singing to *you,* I was singing to the baby." She gestured to Lila's belly. "But if you're going to be cruel about it..." Vivian sullenly walked away and went back to folding laundry.

Lila rolled her eyes and pulled the book that she was actually reading out from inside of the baby book cradled over it. She was trying to find more information about insect migration patterns, anything that could help.

"I'm seeing your therapist today, for a check-in," Vivian called out while loading the dryer. "I'm expecting your room to be clean before I get back. And I expect you to eat the lunch I made for you."

Lila scrunched her face in disgust, not realizing Vivian had already come back.

"Don't look at your mother that way. What's the matter with you?"

"I wasn't," Lila said. "Looking at you. I just…feel heavy. I don't know, like something bad is going to happen."

"Yeah, it will, if you don't eat."

"I don't want to," Lila pressed.

"It's just the baby making you nauseous, sweetheart, but you need to eat." Vivian tried again, feigning sweetness this time.

"Did you know that when you're pregnant, your body produces almost double the amount of blood? I'm carrying so much blood right now. I'm just a bag of blood."

"*Ick!*" Vivian made a disgusted sound. "Don't be so vulgar."

"I'm not. It's just true."

"Where did you learn that? Why would you say that?"

"I read it somewhere."

"Lila, you read too much. It's just upsetting you. I know you like to read, it's why I gave you the baby books."

"I'm not reading too much," Lila said, finding it ironic that this fact is exactly the type of thing she'd read in a baby book. Lila hated this argument, the same one they always had.

"All those books are why you have these issues. You're doing it to yourself," Vivian had said to her once.

This cruel dismissal was something Lila believed for a while. She tried to read more uplifting stories, but to her, there was no truth in those. Romantic fairy tales with happily-ever-afters she could never understand. It wasn't realistic. Some prince to take her away to a glowing castle? What if the prince who shows up doesn't want to save you? What if he wants to hurt you? What if no one ever comes, and you're completely alone? What if every time you escaped a tower, you just stumbled right into a new one? These stories wanted her to believe in a rescuer, but this was impossible for Lila to imagine. Impossible things happened every day, Lila knew this. But not that kind of impossible. At least not for her.

"Well try doing something else, something lighter!" Vivian insisted. "Tell me about your friends at school! Do you ever do anything fun?"

Lila didn't bother to tell her mother she had no friends. "I think reading is fun. Books are my friends."

"Reading is solitary. It's better for you to spend time with people."

"No, it's not. Solitary, I mean. It's the closest connection you can have. With who wrote the book. With the characters. With the book itself."

Vivian grabbed a sweater from the laundry pile. Her phone chimed with a voicemail, and she rested the phone between her ear and shoulder, her hands folding together the ends of the sweater sleeve. While listening, the expression on her face shifted, and Lila got nervous. Vivian immediately called the number and disappeared down the hall to grab another laundry basket.

As she walked back into the living room, she said into the phone, "I'm so sorry. She must have misunderstood. Is there anything else available today? Thank you so much. She will be there. Thank you again."

Vivian hung up and turned to Lila. "You moved your appointment to this morning and then didn't show up? You didn't even bother to cancel it? What were you thinking? They pardoned you for the no-show, only because I rescheduled you for their last available opening today, in an hour."

Lila kept her gaze on the sentence she was reading, not bothering to hide anymore that it wasn't the baby book. "I'm not in labor. Why do I have to go to another appointment?"

"Dammit, Lila!" Vivian snatched the book from her hands and slapped Lila across the face. "Enough! Now you are going to go to that appointment, and you *will* get yourself there on time. Do you understand me? I've had enough of your disrespect! I've been so patient with you! I haven't even been making you come with me to church!"

That's only because you're ashamed of your pregnant daughter, Lila thought. She was stunned by the slap, so she didn't dare say this out loud. She knew better than to talk back.

"You think you're the only one who's afraid? Guess who gets to raise another baby all over again? It's obviously not going to be you." Vivian threw her hands up in frustration. "Get ready for your appointment. The second it's over, meet me at your therapist's office."

LILA SAT IN the lobby of the OBGYN office among the sea of pregnant bellies, some mothers and daughters, most couples, some even accompanied by multiple family members, clearly visible by their resemblance. Lila noticed she was the only one there who had come alone. State law said she was entitled to privacy for her pregnancy appointments, even as a minor. It was only if she wanted an abortion that she needed parental permission. But birth? Allowed. Required, if you came from a family like hers. According to state law, she was old enough to die in childbirth, but not old enough to refuse to die in childbirth. And so, here she was.

She hated being around people, especially in groups. It made her think of the swarms. Normally Lila could read anywhere, but her anxiety would not let her focus. She kept rereading the same sentence over and over, her eyes blurring the lines together. She was woozy. Hungry. Thirsty, too. Drinking water wasn't an option because then she would have to pee and there was nothing grosser than public bathrooms. Then there was the issue that every time she was trapped in a room with a toilet, she wanted to throw up.

She hadn't eaten in…maybe thirty hours? She tried not to count, it made the binges worse. Her hands were shaking, and she reminded herself to fold her hands together so that her doctor, if observant enough, wouldn't notice the small marks from her teeth grating a wound into the top of her knuckles from years of purging. She never really had to come up with excuses for it, no one ever noticed. People were not attentive in that way, Lila realized after a time of worrying about hiding it. If for some reason they ever did see it, she'd tell them it was a scrape. Or some other stupid excuse. But doctors were funny like that, they either missed a major diagnosis that could be responsible for killing you, or knew your medical secrets merely by glancing at you.

"Lila?" a nurse called out to the busy room.

Lila forced herself out of the chair and toward the smiling blonde woman wearing purple scrubs and a loose ponytail.

"Hi, how are you today?" she asked. "Did you make it in safe? Those clouds are scary! It's going to be a crazy monsoon season this year!"

"Yeah, the sky looks pretty ominous," Lila answered politely, apathetic about the weather, about all of this, wanting to get in and out of this place as quickly as possible. To do as her mother instructed. To get this over with, then get away from the hordes of people.

"We're going to be in the third room on the left." The nurse pointed at an ajar door up the hallway, with glaringly shiny floors and a faint chemical smell that was causing a cluster headache to form above Lila's left eyebrow. The nurse followed Lila into the room, sorted through some equipment on a rolling cart next to the seat. When Lila sat on the crinkly paper, she had the uncontrollable urge to scream. She willed herself to remain quiet.

"Here's your gown. Go ahead and put this on, and we'll be right back in for your exam."

For a moment, Lila imagined that in some alternate reality, where she wasn't alone, where the return wasn't real, where none of this was happening, maybe Marcus would be here with her. Maybe her father would've kicked her out, maybe she'd have to live with Marcus. Or maybe he'd leave her too. Maybe both of them would disown her.

She remembered how Marcus reacted to another girl in their grade who got pregnant. "All of these girls are sluts," Marcus said. "You're not like them, Lila," he'd told her, which she knew was meant as an insult. "Yes, I am," she'd retorted, not understanding what he was getting at. But deep down, she knew, it wasn't that she wasn't like other girls, she just wasn't like anyone at all. She was a freak, someone that no one else could ever understand.

Then she felt angry again, at the way he could pervade her thoughts. Her reality was bigger than him now. She could almost feel that sting of bile rising up her throat again. She scanned the room for a sink or trash can, wondering if she was really going to throw up, from nausea this time, not intentionally—she had nothing in her stomach to purge. The last thing she needed was to vomit in here, in front of the photographs of sleeping infants and smiling, exhausted parents with her doctor in full surgical attire. In front of all the cutesy, illustrated art of baby elephants and human babies clutching teddy bears.

The doctor was probably going to comment on how small she was for being so far along, despite her protruding belly. She didn't even feel guilty about any harm she was causing herself or the pregnancy. She knew from research about the risks with bulimia: pancreatitis, acid reflux, esophageal rupture, laryngeal damage, gastrointestinal problems, gum and tooth decay, endocrine abnormalities, sleep disturbances, hair loss, dermatologic symptoms, malnourishment, respiratory arrest, cardiac arrest, sudden death. But she was still alive, so.

I'm fine, she always thought. *I have to get this out.* She never used the word *baby* in her mind. It was just something else she couldn't accept as really happening.

"Excuse me," Lila croaked before the nurse headed out. "Is it all right if I use the bathroom first?"

"Sure, hon. Let me show you where it is. It's down the hall, follow me."

The nurse walked Lila barely a few feet to the next door over, and she told Lila to take her time. Lila inwardly panicked at the invisible filth of this room, the horrors of what may have touched the lid of this toilet, how she normally propped her elbows on the seat at home to purge when she wasn't throwing up in the shower, how much harder this all was with an enormous belly that made her feel like a huge whale and made it impossible to move around or bend down, like she was living through a slowed-down raincloud of misery. She stood for a few seconds, staring at the unfamiliar public toilet. Trying to decide what to do.

She was dizzy. No longer just nauseous, but dizzy, disoriented. She wanted to lie down. When the nausea progressed into black dots clouding her vision, she splashed some water on her face at the sink, didn't dare look at herself in the mirror. She couldn't throw up in here. *What the fuck was I thinking? This place is gross.*

When she creaked opened the door to go back out to the hallway, a front desk employee ran past, and in a hushed shout, "Where's Tina? The exterminator is waiting outside for the termite inspection. He wants to schedule to come back to treat them. Should I sign for her?"

Then it all turned to white noise, and Lila sank into a pit of disgust, thinking of termites burrowing through the walls of this room, how maybe the termites had completely infested a busy place like this where there was no time for anything, everyone too focused on the human breeding while the insect masses were breeding far faster and could easily target her, follow her home. *That's not going to happen*, she tried to tell herself. *You have to stay, or Mom will be pissed.*

Lila stood there, frozen in fear. Then another voice, Tina's, presumably, came chiming up the hallway and said, "Just signed! It's not termites, it's mud wasps."

And Lila started to breathe rheavily. She recalled the exact phrase she wrote in her journal entry that she shared with Dr. Peralta: *I'm being hunted by wasps.* She could suddenly hear that buzzing in the walls, in her head, inside her body, blurring up her vision. In a desperate act of survival, her feet carried her to the nearest exit.

On her way to her car, she saw the exterminator van parked out front beside a red-headed man in a gray uniform, both of which were adorned in lettering that read: *Pest People.* There was a cartoonish, gruesome looking ant painted on the side of the van, and behind it, a rat with red eyes. The nausea came up in a sharp wave, and Lila hunched over and threw up bile in the street.

She wiped her mouth, got into her car and slammed the door, gripping her trembling fingers on the wheel, resisting the urge to stare for too long at the exterminator in her mirrors. She slammed her fists against the steering wheel, accidentally honking the horn. "Marcus! You stupid asshole. How could you do this to me? How could you!" she shouted.

Fumbling around the passenger side of her car, she picked up the journal that had fallen between the seat. She plucked a pen from the cup holder and started writing a letter to Marcus.

Marcus, why did you hurt me? I loved you.

She paused for a minute to gather up her thoughts after noticing his scrawl at the bottom of the page: *No one will save you.*

He was obsessed with this idea, of there being no after-life, only nothingness after death. Lila thought again of her father, rotted in the ground, his soul blacked out from the world, floating in a ceaseless dark. It made her sad. The thought unbearable.

"I know," she whispered to Marcus. "You're right."

She thought of Vivian's harshness, seemingly only caring for the baby, forgetting her own daughter. She thought of Dr. Peralta's nonchalance to just accept the return as if nothing could be done. Lila didn't want to accept the way things were. Lila didn't want this to happen. Why did no one else ever do anything? Then she glanced at the clock on her dashboard, realizing it was almost noon, that she was supposed to meet her mom at Dr. Peralta's. She put the car in reverse, hurrying out of the parking lot.

X

NAZARET WAS EAGER to meet Lila's mother, if a little concerned. Vivian had called her in hysterics about Lila's behavior, and Nazaret wondered if they would need to start regular group sessions.

Vivian entered the office and seated herself on the couch right away, not bothering to introduce herself or share pleasantries. Nazaret noticed how beautiful Vivian was—thin, with elegant posture, very made up, her auburn hair shiny and styled to perfection. She was exactly the type of woman Gabe would fall for.

"So, you mentioned you're having some difficulties with Lila at home?" Nazaret began.

"Yes!" Vivian blurted. "She's just impossible! I don't know what I'm supposed to do with her."

"I see. What are your biggest concerns right now?"

"She's not eating. She's lazy. All she does is read weird books and talk about the end of the world! Nothing I say helps her. I pray for her, but she doesn't get better. I don't want to be a single mother. My husband is dead. My daughter is lost. All she talks about is everyone dying. Now I have to start all over again with this baby."

Nazaret picked up her notepad, a wave of emotion coming over her. *I don't want to be a single mother.* She heard that sentence like a stone in her gut.

"How did your late husband… I'm so sorry, what was his name?"

"Ernesto," Vivian said.

"How was your and Ernesto's relationship when he was alive?"

An uncomfortable laugh erupted from Vivian's throat. "He was not a perfect man, but I loved him."

Nazaret felt the sting of recognition in herself, buried sorrow, acceptance, forgiveness, tolerance for an entire life's worth of devotion that was never returned.

"And his imperfections?"

Vivian shook her head, smiling. "Oh, we don't speak ill of the dead," she said, as if protecting a very important secret, as if God would strike her down for speaking the truth.

"At least when he was alive, Lila would eat. Ernesto liked to cook, he was excellent at it. Lila loved everything he made. He made her breakfast every single day. Chorizo and eggs. Chilaquiles. Anything she wanted. But all of that is so fattening, you know." Vivian said. "Lila can't be eating that right now."

"All of what?" Nazaret asked, interested in hearing about Lila's eating changes.

"All of those foods, Ernesto's foods."

"I'm sorry, what? I don't understand."

"You know, Mexican food."

"You're saying Mexican food is too fattening for Lila to eat? Despite the fact that she likes it?" Nazaret wrote, *Fat shaming Lila. Shaming meals her father fed her.*

"Is this something you've said to Lila?"

"Oh yeah," Vivian continued, oblivious to why this question was being asked. "I mean, it's all meat, cheese, and carbs. A lot on the body. Especially for her, she's growing a baby. She doesn't need to make it harder, carrying more fat around. It's not nutritious for a fetus."

"And when did Lila's difficulties with food begin, that you can remember?"

Vivian didn't get to answer, because Lila walked in the office, arriving from her obstetrics appointment. She crossed her arms, clearly uncomfortable with having to be in the same room with both her mother and her therapist.

"Hello, Lila, nice to see you," Nazaret said, but Lila didn't respond.

Vivian didn't greet her daughter and patted at the empty space next to her on the couch. Once Lila sat, Vivian continued, going back to the conversation about Ernesto's cooking. "He took pride it in it. In taking care of us. He felt it was his duty as a man, being head of the household."

Nazaret didn't comment on that statement. Instead, she asked, "Who's head of your household now?"

Vivian didn't like this question and just stared back at Nazaret, as if offended. "Well, I am, of course. And we are a God-fearing home. So, the Lord is first. He guides me to lead our family the way Ernesto would have."

Nazaret nodded, not commenting on Vivian's beliefs. "Your nails are quite beautiful," she said, observing that Vivian was very mindful of appearances. "What happened to your finger?" she asked, noticing part of Vivian's left pinky was amputated, only a half-stub remaining.

"Oh, caught it in a door," Vivian answered dismissively.

Lila rolled her eyes and spoke for the first time since she entered the room. "You mean when Dad threw you out and slammed the door so hard on your pinky that they had to amputate the top knuckle?"

"Lila!" Vivian chastised, mortified at the reveal of this information.

Nazaret noticed the same pride in Vivian that she'd seen in many abused women. She saw right through it, the shield needed to cement their strength. The potent fear of her husband was less apparent, with his death. But the pride, the shame, that's not something that ever seemed to go. No matter how many years passed. Whatever changed for these women, that never did.

"I am very sorry that happened to you," Nazaret said, to both of them, starting to piece together gaps in Lila's life that she had previously suspected. Nazaret didn't know how to address Vivian's denial, her confusion of how to exist in the world as a widow still bowing to an abuser's ghost.

"Lila, next session, I would like for us to start implementing some mindfulness practices and CBT to start to tackle—" she made a point not to say *eating disorder treatments*—"the difficulties you're having with daily routines, so you can feel your best for when the baby gets here. I will be in contact with some other health professionals, but we'll get through this, okay?"

Lila just nodded, clearly not caring at all.

Nazaret hated these moments, witnessing suffering that made her mute out or compare her own, reasoning that at least her life wasn't this bad. At least Gabe never laid a hand on her. It could always be worse. Men could always do and be worse. Even dead men left injuries in their absence, a jarring silence after their violence and cruelty carved gaps resembling presence—gaps that looked like love, that clutched onto families for generations to keep repeating.

"Vivian, it was nice to meet you. I appreciate the initiative you're both taking." This slipped out of Nazaret's mouth, like it did with many clients. She doubted either of them would be making leaps toward change.

Nazaret thought about how much she hated being a healer sometimes. Everyone's suffering too impossible to carry, nursing others' wounds until hers were slowly zipping open, a gaping abyss trying to swallow her in one ragged breath.

XI

NAZARET COULDN'T ADMIT to herself that she had started to worry about this bottomless hunger, a yearning she couldn't satiate. Nothing was enough lately. She wondered if it was possible to have a craving for something you've never eaten.

Nazaret turned to her computer, ignoring her overflowing inbox of emails and the ungodly amount of documents she had to deal with. She clicked through some YouTube rabbit hole, watching videos of people cooking and eating both live and dead locusts, crickets, and scorpions. Her new obsession, Lila's constant commentary about insects bleeding into her subconscious.

She clicked on a video titled *Chapulines Made Easy*, in which some smiling man was smashing up toasted grasshoppers in a molcajete and mixing them into guacamole, and then she watched another video of shouting Americans at various Chinese and Vietnamese food markets, filming themselves eating live scorpions. A woman grabbed a staked scorpion, the arachnid still moving, then brought it to her mouth, its tail weakly trying to sting her lip in one final fight for its doomed life. Nazaret imagined how acerbic it must taste. In another video, hands gripped fistfuls of live grasshoppers and dropped them into boiling water. The cook then strained and seasoned them, transferring them to a pan, some still twitching while being drizzled in sauce at the same time. This part was her favorite, the preparing, the waiting, the anticipation before the eating. The buzz inside of her grew to a roaring. She felt wired. Awake. Alive.

Dazed, she noticed tons of sticky notes littered all over her desk. Notes scribbled in names. All the baby names she had written down that she liked. *Anastasia. Gerald. Diego. Jonathan. Mary.* Each on their own note, stuck in a separate area, to be visible and regarded with equal care. Nazaret was overwhelmed by realizing that she didn't remember doing that, but didn't want to bother with that now. Her attention quickly returned to the videos, the pull of them intoxicating.

She figured that she really could eat anything, that she might eat and never stop. That maybe she needed to try mukbang or eating contests. *I'm so hungry. I have to stop watching this. Should I get a cheeseburger? No, I want tacos. I want seasoned locusts, tostadas, scorpions on a stick. I want…* She had an urge to feel mastication, to stick her mandibles in something, to grip it with her maxillae, to drag the food along her labial and maxillary palps, to bite into the hard resistance of an exoskeleton.

She went back to her open tab of Google search results, not remembering what the hell she was even looking up when she had typed in *find mates*, her eyes drawn to an article called, "Female Desert Locust Mating Habits: Multiple Mating Increases Egg Weight," published in an entomology journal called *The Desert Entomologist.* This was one of the first results on the page, the algorithm already learning her after watching the insect videos.

Scanning through the article, she read details about egg size and biomass, the sexual selection of locust females, outlining the benefits of polyandry and multiple mates on reproductive success. Another article from the same journal detailed a preference for salt and protein in the diet, that when swarming, locusts prefer cannibalizing the same species over other insect corpses. This was something Nazaret realized she already knew but didn't understand how. Probably something Lila had told her.

Her eyes wandered to her desk, at the framed photo of her two smiling children, more names written on notes pasted all around the picture frame. For a minute, she studied their familiar, unfamiliar faces, even their names escaping her. There were so many names to remember now. So many people to take care of. Too many.

THAT NIGHT, NAZARET found herself on the couch, illuminated in the haze of the dim light on the television because she couldn't sleep. Stephen King and George A. Romero's *Creepshow* was blaring on the TV, and she was transfixed, watching the anthology chapter episode of a man being consumed by cockroaches.

Gabe stumbled in, half-asleep, snatching for the remote to turn it down. "What the hell is the matter with you? It's late. Why are you even watching this?" he snapped at her in disgust. He pressed the remote over and over, frustrated that it wasn't working. Then he charged over to the TV, swatted at the power button, and the screen went black.

Nazaret rolled her eyes. This opened a corner of her brain at how much squeamish men annoyed her. She reasoned that women were so accustomed to blood, to constant fear of bodily harm, to the fine line between death, birth, and cyclic regeneration, that these fragile types of men were weak.

Once he retreated, she immediately turned it back on, letting it play on mute, drifting in and out of sleepiness.

In the morning, after fumbling through her mother motions on autopilot and taking her kids to school, she poured a mug of black coffee and seated herself across from Gabe at the table.

It occurred to Nazaret in this moment that something felt very wrong. "I think maybe my sleeping pills are messing with me," she told Gabe. "I'm having crazy dreams or something. It's like I can't sleep at all anymore, and when I do, or if I think I'm asleep, everything is dream-like but I *feel* awake, and I'm exhausted. I remember these absurd moments, the haze of night, of being in bed, but then in the morning it's all fog, this confusion. Then these fuzzy images come through, like my memory has fused into the subconscious world of my dreams, or of…something else. I'm always starving. I feel like a zombie lately. I'm all animal. Last night, I think I was sleepwalking? Did I get out of bed?"

"That's weird," Gabe said without concern, not bringing up the television incident. "You've been taking those sleeping pills for months now. Don't you think you would have noticed something sooner? You didn't have any side effects before. Now that you mention it, you've been having night terrors or something though."

"I have? Why didn't you tell me?"

"I don't know." He shrugged. "Sometimes you rustle around, murmuring, probably having nightmares. I forgot about it until right now. Isn't the rule not to wake someone in the middle of a sleep episode or something?"

"You *forgot* to mention it? Really? So, I'm just not fucking important enough to remember then, is that it?" she yelled, rising in anger and getting ready to leave the table.

"Oh, Jesus, here we go," he responded coolly, acting annoyed but also like he didn't care enough to argue.

As she stood, a praying mantis skittered out from behind the chair leg, directly beside Gabe's foot. Startled, she spilled coffee on herself, gritting her teeth at the burn.

"You're so jumpy," he said and laughed. "It's just a praying mantis. Look, he's praying. Nothing scary about that."

Nazaret wiped at the stain on her shirt and ignored him, pissed off at his dismissal of the mantis, of everything, but more reeling from some deep-seated terror she couldn't contain, realizing she wanted to throw herself through the nearest window, to escape, to flee this life, or to run a shard of glass along her wrist, to peel off this skin, leave it behind. Go anywhere else.

"Goddammit, Gabe!" she shouted and smashed her fist onto the table, accidentally slamming it into the mug, catching it just right and causing it to shatter. Porcelain pierced into the side of her fist, and she pulled out two large shards, revealing a bleeding gash that might need stitches, a necessity she would ignore. She shrieked, pulling her hand away on impulse of pain. Then she turned her wrist slowly to assess the damage, watching the blood pour out of her wound with detached curiosity. She silently held out her fingers to Gabe, and he inhaled through his teeth.

"Ouch. Here let me..." he said, trying for an excuse to leave.

She shook her head no.

"No?" he asked, confused. "What do you want me to do?"

She shoved her hand in his face, then up to his lips.

"You want me to kiss it?" he laughed uncomfortably. "Who do I look like, Gomez Addams?" He was disgusted by the blood, doing a terrible job of hiding it.

"Just do it," she said, and held them up to his lips again. Waiting.

He seemed fearful she would smear the blood all over his mouth, eyeing her with suspicion, trying to decipher what was wrong with her, if this was a sex thing, a loss of sanity thing, a joke.

"Can you just…"

"What? You want me to drink your blood now? Nazaret, you're scaring me," he snapped.

He gripped her hand and yanked it toward him. She wanted him to hold it tenderly, not like a brute.

He examined the wound. "Yeah, this is deep. I don't know what you want from me," he said dismissively. "Looks bad though. You should go to urgent care or something," he said, not offering to drive her.

Nazaret knew this man was a parasite, one too weak to even take her blood. To handle the realities of life, of commitment, of anything.

Suddenly she wanted to find a vial, squeeze the blood out of her wound, fill it, force it down his throat. She wanted to fly free into this world, see who would take it willingly.

She got up and brushed past him, struggling to navigate even walking through the hallway, a blaring alarm ringing through her nervous system. Rage pounded through her veins, the blood dripping along her wrist, leaving a pattering trail that followed her down the hall.

Fumbling through the medicine cabinet for something to wrap it, she didn't find much. Only things for her kids. Checking her watch, she didn't have time to go anywhere anyway, reasoning she might as well just go to work, and if bleeding got worse, deal with it later. She ran the wound under water, then dumped hydrogen peroxide over it, not even flinching at the bubbles that burned far worse than when the shards tore open her flesh. She sloppily wrapped a bandage over it, wondering if she should attempt to at least Google the right way to do it, then realized she didn't give a shit. Blood seeped through the gauze, but she just wrapped another layer over it.

On a stress impulse, Nazaret went back to the kitchen, looking for something to eat. When she opened the pantry, it was empty. There were only crumbs. She remembered the hazy image of seeing her children in here. Then her life flashed before her in one long fever dream—from egg to nymph to—*Wait, why am I thinking about it like that? With that…terminology?*

XII

LILA DOUBLE-CHECKED THAT her door was locked and climbed back on her bed, surrounded by bags of chips. She was carefully licking each one, sucking the salt off and then spitting the saltless soggy chip back out into a separate bag. She had already amassed an entire graveyard of chewed-up pretzels, having spit them out too without swallowing them. This way was easiest, because it felt like eating, but she could cheat her way out of it—get the taste without any of the downside.

She turned to the mountain of books on her bed, trying to decide which one to read. Marcus had scrawled all over them, always attempting to deter her from having her own thoughts. Still deciding, she reached for the Bible, attempting to read it while also trying to ignore the memory of her and Marcus's last fight. She could still feel him leering over her shoulder, snatching the book from her hands.

"You believe in this shit?"

"I'm just researching," Lila said.

"Isn't this the same ghost in the sky who sent the waves of locusts you're so afraid of? The one who just watched during genocides? Same one who flooded the Earth? Yeah, let's ask him. You think he cares? You think he'll save you?"

"I'm not trying to be saved." Lila said, defensive. "I'm trying to help everyone else."

He laughed. "Well good luck with that." He thumbed through the pages, examining her sticky notes. "You've got this unshakable faith inside of you, hanging on every word in these fucking books. Why do you let them hold so much power over you, huh? You've surrendered your entire being to this shit. You're here, but you're not here." He tapped at his head, signaling she was not sane. "It's crazy, the way you are. I've been with you for a decade, and even I can't figure out what's the matter with you."

Lila had said nothing to this, just waited for him to be through. She hated how his opinions of her affected her so much.

After a pause, he continued. "In a weird way, I get it. That logic, killing us. This world is totally fucked. If he gave a shit at all, he'd just put us out of our misery."

He set the Bible down among her dystopic novels.

"You and your dystopias," he said, rummaging through the pile of them.

Along with Kafka's *The Metamorphosis*, Lila's stack of *Fahrenheit 451, 1984, Brave New World*, and others, were grouped together for the dystopic literature elective she had taken.

"These books belong over here," he said, moving her religious texts to the stack. "Religion was the original dystopia. Ancient peoples who worshiped many gods were even afraid of the sun, refusing to go outside during an eclipse, fearing its wrath. Religion has been preaching our untimely deaths as a selling point since time immemorial, that we'll be cast down by fire in the sky if we don't just obey. But let me let you in on a little secret. The world is always ending, Lila. Every day is a dystopia for somebody." He stopped for a second to adjust the tower of books so it wouldn't fall over.

Lila thought about everything he'd just said, plagued by the image of when they met, him holding that magnifying glass in the sun, burning the ants below.

"Maybe today it's the end of some civilization," he went on. "War. Genocide. Natural disasters. Or as this fairy tale collection might call it," he said, snatching The Holy Bible and waving it in her face, "acts of God. For all of us, it's coming. Probably sooner than we think. Nothing in here will tell you anything new. But you already know this. You just want someone to prove you right. You know who you should believe in, Lila? Yourself. Whichever god you pick, whatever story, it doesn't matter. It's all just a thought experiment. In the end, it's the same. Everyone dies."

He rifled through the stack some more, noticing a copy of Arthur C. Clarke's collection *The Nine Billion Names of God.* "This is an amazing story, actually," he confessed.

Lila braved turning to look at him. "It's my favorite short story. Ever."

"I know," he said gently. "Not all of these books are pointless rabbit holes. You just stress me out so much. I hate when you make me like this," he said, reverting again to a cruel tone. "What is it that all these books have in common, Lila?"

"They're written by men," she answered immediately, without thinking.

He stopped, surprised, not expecting that answer.

"All those books," she said as she pointed at the stack, those get assigned at school—those grand, epic, ends of the world tales. All narratives of huge devastations. But I don't know..." Lila quieted. "Sometimes, I think it's a lot smaller. More intimate. Something subtle, not obviously threatening, at first. Insidious in a different way than just wars or angry gods. More invisible, familiar. Weaponry and violence aren't the only way to destroy a society. It can suffocate from within, so slowly and effectively that no one notices until it's too late."

Lila glanced at the tattered cover of her copy of Clarke sitting on her nightstand now, and took a deep breath. Then she looked to her copies of *The Memory Police, The Power, The Handmaid's Tale*—dystopias that her class failed to cover, ones she related to more. She tried to block Marcus out, refusing him from overtaking her present moment. Her father's voice was fighting in her head too, insisting she must obey God, feeling the heaviness of the Bible in her lap. She thumbed the sticky note sticking out the gilded pages and opened to a passage that she kept obsessing over.

Hosea 13:14–16

13   "I will deliver this people from the power of the grave;
       I will redeem them from death.
       Where, O death, are your plagues?
       Where, O grave, is your destruction?

       "I will have no compassion…

15   even though he thrives among his brothers.
       An east wind from the LORD will come,
       blowing in from the desert;
       his spring will fail
       and his well dry up.
       His storehouse will be plundered
       of all its treasures.

¹⁶   The people of Samaria must bear their guilt,
        because they have rebelled against their God.
        They will fall by the sword;
        their little ones will be dashed to the ground,
        their pregnant women ripped open."

She highlighted the section that read, *an east wind from the LORD will come, blowing in from the desert.* Then a sting of pins and needles crept over her when she got to that last line. She had already underlined it in red marker, which made the whole passage more grotesque, the bloody imagery real. *Their pregnant women ripped open.*

She remembered all those years of oscillating between a state of mindless obedience and terror because that's what her father expected of her. To be a good Catholic girl. To make sure her entire life had been crushed by the weight of the words in this book.

Though the words felt hollow, the details here terrified her. She wondered how much of this biblical history was going to mirror the return, if it could help her figure out what to do, the way her parents always said God would help.

She couldn't stop thinking about that line about pregnant women. A rush of despair consumed her. Reaching for the pretzel bag, she sucked the salt off of the last one and crumbled the bag to throw it away.

This was a prime attractant for insects, so she made sure to double bag the masticated slop before burying the evidence in the guts of the trash. After discarding it in the kitchen, Lila heard a vehicle pull up to the house. She peered out of the living room window. A van was parked outside, with a cartoon ant in front of a cartoon rat painted on the side panel. It was *the* van. The one from the OBGYN office: *Pest People.*

And it was even the exact same man. Red hair, scruffy beard, same logo on his gray shirt. Lila almost started to hyperventilate but ran and hid when she heard the doorbell. *Why is he here? Is he following me?* Then she could hear muffled conversation at the front door, realizing that her mother had let this man inside their home.

Lila emerged from down the hall, stopping in the entryway. The sight of him made her feel faint, stirring up the terror she felt around exterminators, despite knowing that in a way, they served her mission, to keep the insects out. Her arrival interrupted their conversation.

"Lila, go to your room," Vivian said dismissively and turned back to the exterminator. "Don't mind my daughter, she is extremely phobic about bugs, and she gets upset. That's actually why I called you. In our bathroom there's been a few roaches, and we've also had a lot of cicadas this year. And now, there's locusts. They're all over the yard suddenly. My daughter is even convinced there is one lone wasp living outside her window." Her voice trailed off down the hall as she led the exterminator through the house and to the backyard.

Lila pressed her ear against the sliding glass window. *Locusts?* She hadn't seen any when she was cleaning her windowsill. Vivian must have decided to not tell her about them. She could hear the exterminator's voice well enough, though it was muffled. But his words came through clear.

"You've got a lot of insect activity out here," he said, his voice gruff, vocal cords trashed from years of chain smoking. "I can pour something down the drains in the bathrooms, though you'll need a plumber to clean everything out if it's giving you any backup. Sometimes organic waste lines the pipes and attracts them, so they start coming up. As for these grasshoppers, this could easily become an infestation. They can turn up in droves this time of year. You might try some mantis egg farms to combat this. It's real fun to watch." He laughed a gurgling laugh that nearly turned to a wheeze. "Try not to agitate them, if you can help it," he went on. "When they get in a flurry and start to swarm, they cannibalize each other in the frenzy. They'll eat all your plants, destroy everything. Themselves, too. It's sick. Now, I'm happy to spray your existing hoppers, but this time of year? They're in the middle of a reproductive cycle, so you'll get another swath of them coming up with a vengeance. Their cycles are relentless. Eat, breed, swarm. Usually they'll just circle the first two, but watch out if they get aggressive. They can be unpredictable. You'll see an increase in their visibility after our first treatment, once they come out of hiding. Even if this round dies off, they're not gone. They'll be back. Especially if they've got a fresh water source. How often are you using this irrigation system out here?"

They turned the corner to another area of the yard, and Lila lost his voice. Hearing all of this tormented her. Still, she waited, unable to stop listening.

After a few moments of nothing, his muffled voice returned when they rounded the corner again. "Good thing you called. This gets out of control fast. The cicadas and grasshoppers will attract their own predators. Might get big spiders coming around if you don't have them already. Or scorpions. Rodents, too. Then you get the snakes coming after the rodents. Coyotes and mountain lions coming after the snakes. I recommend we spray right now because without taking action on this, it'll become a never-ending cycle of everything killing everything."

As he said this, a fly hummed past Lila's face and landed at the corner of the sliding door. She shrieked and ducked to the ground, reflexively covering her head. *He let a fly in.*

This upset her immensely. It had been a serious problem back when they still had Rocco their Mastiff, when flies would inevitably make their way inside whenever the dog had to go out. Seeing this fly now made Lila run through the hall to make sure all the doors were closed so it wouldn't get lost somewhere in the house, especially her bedroom. She closed her door and hid under the comforter in bed, trying to escape the fly, thinking of how much she had loved Rocco, how devastated she was to lose him.

She remembered that summer with him, their only summer together, how the flies swarmed worse than ever, how she had tried to protect him when the flies would gather on his ears.

"Get off of him!" she'd screamed, lunging toward Rocco frantically, and the dog had lowered his head in apology, as if Lila was yelling at him. "No! Not you, I'm sorry. I wasn't yelling at you. It was the flies." He seemed to understand, inching forward to lick her face. She'd petted him, swatting at the air to make sure nothing came back to land on him, to infest him. It terrified her when he went outside, where the mosquitoes and ticks and fleas could bring blood-borne disease.

Sure enough, they didn't have the dog long. Rocco mysteriously "went to heaven" a few weeks later, possibly ran over by the neighbor's F350, something Lila didn't think Vivian would ever tell the truth about. Lila hated her for this. This incident felt divinatory, an evolving pattern, evidence of the darkness that flies brought.

In her bedroom, safe from the current fly for the time being, Lila peered out of the blinds, watching the exterminator work. Beholding him, he looked almost like a skeleton, a grim reaper, his silver canister of poison with that cord sprayer his long scythe. As he approached Lila's window to spray around the outside of it, he waved at her, and in that instant, she saw a flash of death in his eyes, a reflection of her own demise. Terror took hold of her, and a horrible cramp surged through her womb that made her wince and inhale sharply in pain. Lila knew that her time was running out. Soon, they would be here. And they would be mad.

XIII

NAZARET'S HEADACHE KEPT intensifying, despite the pill concoction she had dry-swallowed twenty minutes ago. These new migraines had been incessant, but she didn't want to take a sick day because being at home was worse than this. The stinging in her hand was present, but the wrapping was holding fine, and she was successfully ignoring it otherwise.

Right on time, Lila entered the office, belly full and sitting low, a beach ball against her small frame. She was completely covered in denim, wearing long sleeves and pants, as well as an oversized hat with attached mosquito cloth. Only her hands were exposed.

What in God's green earth is this child wearing?

"That's quite the ensemble you've got on today," Nazaret commented as Lila sat on the couch. "Aren't you hot?"

Lila lifted the mesh fabric up, showing her face. "If you're going to make fun of me, then I'll—"

"I'm not making fun of you. I'm simply pointing out the very interesting outfit you're wearing in the middle of summer. Did you get stung by something? What happened?"

Lila draped the mesh back down, letting it cover her. "I saw a mosquito in my room last night, so I put on the heaviest denim jacket I have and jeans. Luckily, these still fit. They protect me, despite the heat. The Zika virus is worse, a much bigger threat. Not to mention malaria. West Nile. There's a lot more."

"I see," Nazaret said, her voice dipping into annoyance. "And what is that on your head?"

Lila's floppy black hat had endured a surgery with mosquito netting sloppily sewn into the lining, draping over her face like some kind of mourning veil, but she looked more like a runaway bride that had escaped an asylum. "Mosquitoes kill," Lila said with urgency. "All it takes is one bad bite, and you've contracted a fatal disease. I want to be safe." Lila dug into her purse for a mosquito spray, then started to douse herself in it. A fog of repellent surrounded her.

"Lila!" Nazaret scolded, the smell of it making her head throb. A harsh sting of pain stabbed at the edge of her temples. "That can't be safe for your baby. And you cannot spray anything in here. I have a strict no-fragrance policy. I'm going to have to ask you to put that away, please. Your symptoms are worsening, it seems. Did something happen last week?"

"Everything is the same, I guess. I don't get why I have to come here. This is pointless."

"I understand that you're feeling hopeless right now—" Nazaret pulled out her notes to write, struggling to do so with the wound on her hand. *OCD symptoms worsening. Paranoia severe.* "But you are about to give birth. It's crucial that we keep your health on track as much as we can before the big change of having an infant in your life. When is your due date again?" she asked.

Lila stared at Nazaret's bandaged hand for a second, but didn't comment on it. Nazaret looked down to see spots of blood leaking through the gauze. She ignored it as well.

"October 27ᵗʰ, but I don't think we have that long," Lila said. "Every day, I don't even know if tomorrow will come. I think they'll be here before then."

"Not even a month away. And when you say 'they'… You mean the insects? You believe the masses of insects will come before your delivery? Is that right?" Nazaret paused. A pregnant pause. "Is it possible that this paranoia you're experiencing is a response to your fear about childbirth? The dread of having to undergo the pain? This apocalypse you're fearing being the end of your life as you know it?"

"It's not a fear response, I'm stating a fact. And of course I feel dread. Of course I'm afraid. What do you want me to say?"

Nazaret pursed her lips, considering whether to comment on Lila's attitude, deciding against it. "Today I want to talk about some coping tools we can implement to prepare for the birth of your baby, so that—"

Lila interrupted. "Did you know a scorpion mother gives birth to tons of live young and carries them on her back? They all pile on and cling, never leaving until they are big enough to molt. Isn't that disgusting?"

"Lila, it's important that we pay attention to our goals for the day."

"I am. I'm just saying. I can't imagine how hard that is, having multiples."

Nazaret wanted to snap at Lila and had to refrain herself. *Keep it together, you're in session.* She put on her best therapist voice. "Remember, we don't have much time. A miracle is about to occur. The miracle of birth. And it will change you. You'll see. All you've endured, all you've suffered. You'll emerge anew through this metamorphosis."

"What?" Lila asked sharply.

"I said you'll emerge anew through your metamorphosis of becoming a mother."

"Don't say that to me."

"Please tell me what I said that has upset you."

"You know what you said," Lila snapped, her scowling expression cloaked by the veil.

In some weird glitch, Nazaret's computer started blaring, playing one of the YouTube videos she had left open of the insects.

"What is that?" Lila asked after an uncomfortable pause.

Nazaret got up, but she didn't mute the video or shut it off, just turned the monitor so that Lila could see. The screen displayed zoomed-in footage of an entire bowl of toasted grasshoppers being drenched in lime juice and salt.

When she saw this, Lila froze in revulsion, paralyzed into horrified silence. After a few seconds, she turned away, shrinking into the couch. Nazaret was surprised at how well Lila was holding it together, considering. Surprised at herself, even. That she didn't care at all that this was happening. Unprofessional? Maybe with another client. But with Lila? This was perfect. *We'll call it exposure therapy.*

"Why are you watching this? Are you trying to test me? What is this?" Lila asked, struggling to get the words out, like she was caught between about to cry and about to start yelling.

"Lila, in Mexico and other areas of the world, it is not uncommon to eat insects. Do you have a problem with our culture?" Nazaret asked.

In the video, a man spooned the grasshopper corpses, then started sprinkling them into a taco.

"Why would you even say that? Of course I don't. My fear of insects, my knowing of what's to come, none of that has anything to do with culture. The only problem I have with anything is that we're all going to fucking die!"

"Have you ever tried one?" Nazaret asked, struggling to disguise the eagerness in her voice.

"What are you talking about?!" Lila screamed.

"Here…" Nazaret pulled out a colorful plastic bag of gummy worms she had stuffed in her desk drawer. Lila's face paled as Nazaret shoveled the sugary worms into her mouth, biting the heads off the worms. She had been hoarding these, another step closer to eating the real thing. She extended out the bag and offered it to Lila. "Try one."

Lila covered her nose as if she smelled earth and rot, as if Nazaret's teeth were gnashing live worm heads while their squirming bodies writhed, sludge coming out of them. Lila burst into tears, then rushed over to the corner trash like she might vomit. "You're going to make me have a panic attack!" She tilted her face into the crook of her elbow and gagged. "Why would you do that to me?" Lila sobbed into her hands. "I thought you wanted to help me! I thought you were different! You're just like everyone else!"

"Do the gummy worms upset you?" Nazaret used a tone that made it clear she was losing all patience, all empathy. She realized she really didn't care about this angsty teenage bullshit anymore. That she didn't care about anything. "I will put them away if you wish, but I need you to answer one question for me. Why are the insects coming back? What do they want?"

Lila covered her mouth and nose with her palm and demanded Nazaret dispose of the bag in another room, another galaxy. Frantically, Lila got up to leave. On her way out, she stopped in the doorway, glaring at Nazaret, and growled at her the answer.

"Revenge."

XIV

LILA HURRIED DOWN the street still crying, scaring the few people who bothered to even notice her as she passed. She didn't want to drive herself home right away, didn't feel the need to tell her mother about the appointment, how it was useless, how this stupid doctor didn't believe her either, how no one ever listened. She trudged past the medical plaza and surrounding businesses to the historic district downtown, a few blocks south. She noticed the birds sitting atop the telephone wires, the sun shining, people passing by in anonymous whirs, painfully ignorant of what was to come.

Up the street, the ornate gables and stained-glass windows of the Holy Trinity Cathedral glimmered in the sunlight. Lila admired the towering gothic presence of this ancient building, how it commanded attention. She headed toward it, debating if she should go inside. As she considered this, a fly zoomed past her head, and she frantically waved her arms to keep it away.

Beside her, a dead raccoon lay on the side of the road, covered with flies and maggots. Its bloated belly was overflowing with grub worms. Either it had been hit by a car, ripped open by something trying to eat it, or burst from the gaseous pressure of its own rotting guts. Maybe it died by way of some horrible illness. It had been there a while, baking in the sun.

She coughed and brought her hand to cover her nose, choking at the smell of rotting animal carcass. As she rushed past, the flies noticed and tried to communicate with her. One buzzed near the mesh over her face, almost landing on it. A frantic scream wanted to emerge from her throat. She instantly thought of the fly that flew near her father's shoulder in the last memory she had of him, the image that consumed her.

Memory overtook her of the last conversation they had. The way her brain blocked out what he was saying because there was a fly whirring around, and she had to hide her fixation on it because her father didn't tolerate her behavior around insects. His words were sliding together in distorted mumbles, as she was only focused on the fly. Flies made her sick. They were the worst of all. Even worse than anything with venom, than the violent ones with stingers and pincers, than webs, worse than the slithering ones with no legs.

It had finally landed on the coffee table, with its slow humming like rot making her want to die. That sound. That never-ending droning, like poison toxifying her nervous system, a lute playing some torturous noise to lure victims to its dead pied piper song, an incantation to summon the dregs from an underworld. The sound that said, *I feast on filth. I am the crown of decay. Death is near.*

After that morning, she had proof the insects were trying to tell her something. That they always had a message. Her father had died an hour later, killed on impact when he was T-boned by a drunk driver running a red light. The fly, another omen. Just like with Rocco.

She thought it was a kind of divination she was tapping into, entomancy to be exact. She had been trying to get several difficult-to-acquire books on the subject but was too afraid of what she might read even in her *Entomancy for Beginners* paperback.

Then Lila remembered the other fly that was on her father's casket. What did it want? It rubbed its filthy hands together in an almost act of mockery, as if it could read her thoughts, like it knew that she knew, that she was part of all of this. How one day, she would witness their revival. The pallbearers had stood gloomily whizzing away the flies around their head, waiting in the hot sun like grim statues before walking her father's corpse across the pathway to the hearse.

Those images haunted her, the somber mourners, the crying, her mother's wailing, the incessant sniffling with tissue boxes everywhere, the constant kneeling, the repeating prayers, the old woman playing gothic death music on the pipe organ—but the only real detail Lila could vividly remember about that day was the fucking flies. She had been petrified one would lay eggs on her father's body, that during the wake when someone tried kissing his cold, dead forehead, the corners of his eyes would already be spewing with maggots. That his whole body had gone to spoil, that the insects already had him in their grasp. Because of this, she didn't even look at his open casket. She couldn't bear to.

She remembered kneeling, then standing several times, reciting the prayers over and over, her family clutching rosaries with their heads bowed, her tía squeezing Lila's hand until she thought she might break her wrist. Lila was frozen in shock during the funeral, but cried harder than she'd ever cried in her life that night, her head throbbing like a knife went through it, almost as bad as the pain from the blood vessel she burst in her left eye when she stuck her fingers down her throat and vomited too violently until her esophagus was burned raw. This had occurred three weeks after the service, when she puked for hours straight until all she could feel inside was the dizzying scream of emaciation, barely able to stand up, to swallow, to breathe. She wanted everything to go away. She wanted to disappear.

Trapped in a fog of memory, having finally escaped the raccoon carcass fly cloud, she wiped the remnants of tears from under the mesh and found that her feet had carried her up the steps, through the ornate doors, and she had entered the cathedral.

Looking around, she admired the decorum of the room, the columns, oak seating, the choir stalls, the quiet, terrifying beauty of this building. Angels and statues peered down at her.

When she entered the confession box, she didn't know what she would say. There were no other penitents in line, the entire place was empty. If she didn't know better, she would think she was alone. She kneeled, with some difficulty due to her belly.

Even though she could never tell anyone this, Lila did not consider herself religious, only afraid. She crossed herself. "In the name of the Father, the Son, and the Holy Spirit… Bless me Father, for I have sinned," she began. "It has been nine months since my last confession. I have lied to my mother, police, everyone—and I force myself to throw up every day. I am also pregnant due to premarital sex. Most horrible of all, Father, I have an awful sin for which I must repent, and no one can ever know."

"My child, the Lord already knows. He sees all. But Our Father forgives all," the priest said.

The certainty of this comment made Lila nervous. She fidgeted and looked at the distortions of his face through the other side of the grille. "I don't know, Father. I'm not sure what happened. It's like I couldn't control myself, like I didn't have a say over my actions."

"Go on, my child." The Father's voice was gentle, strangely trustworthy. Even though Lila was apprehensive, for some reason, she felt he wanted to help her. Maybe in this anonymous box, with someone who couldn't tell on her, who could barely see her face covered in mesh and blurred through a screen, maybe it was okay to confess. If there was a God, maybe he really did already know.

"It's difficult to speak about," Lila's voice trembled. "I don't have anyone to talk to and I'm not good at sharing. My mom forced me to go to this therapist who was supposed to help, but she turned out to be horrible. And I just... Thank you for listening." She sniffled, nervous to say everything out loud. The Father waited patiently, and she forced herself to continue.

"It happened the night when my boyfriend Marcus took my virginity. I didn't know what I thought it would be like, not this. I overheard some girls at school saying that sex hurts, and it did, but they didn't say it would bring me these intense feelings, these flashes of rage. I couldn't contain the hatred I had for him. I had to be rid of him, of all of it. They were buzzing louder than ever." Lila's voice cracked, her words closing in on her in the surrounding silence.

"I don't really remember what happened next." She quieted to almost a whisper. "I've tried to grasp at the pieces of it in my memory, I only have flashes." Lila paused, trying to stifle a wave of emotions coming up, all of it coming back.

"My hands were red. Blood everywhere, the walls, my shirt, my legs, the floor, the doorknob. He just lay there in the tub, not moving. I couldn't understand what I was looking at, what I was even doing there half-dressed, half-crazed, covered in guts and blood in the middle of the night, and I began to feel insatiable, like I had never eaten before and never would again. Sort of the way I feel before a binge—that agony when I can't take it any longer. But this was different, beyond compulsion. A power I had no control over, like something possessed me.

"Next thing I know, I'm hacking him up. Went to the kitchen and pulled out a cleaver, the big heavy ones that slice through bone, and I started with a pinky, just for a taste. It scared me, at first. I tried to stop, to find something else—anything—and I devoured everything in the kitchen: peanut butter, cereals, chips, ice cream, bread. It wasn't the same. I couldn't get the flavor of him out of my mouth. So, I sat over him all night, gorging myself. When there was nothing left, I licked his blood off the carpet.

"That's when I felt myself expanding. I went to the kitchen, and I was so full, I could barely move. I could feel the pieces of him sitting right at the top of my throat, the filth of him still inside me. It was almost how I felt when he was on top of me, the heaviness of him squishing me flat like I was nothing. Like I was one of the roaches he used to make me watch him smash to death. It felt like I was invisible, like there was nothing I could do. About any of it. All of it was overwhelming. All of it was coming up.

"I thought I would throw up and ran to the sink. The counter was covered with ants, and so I flew into a rage. I started smashing them with my fists, killed them all. I didn't mean to. Then I cried because I had to touch them, and because I remembered how Marcus would always burn them, all those years ago…"

There was a drawn-out silence on both sides of the screen, but Lila didn't wait. Before the Father could respond, she got up and ran, hauling herself awkwardly down the cathedral hall, past the pews, and out through the large ornate doors.

Outside and out of breath, Lila gasped for a moment and looked up to the darkening sky. Her hand shielded her eyes, and she adjusted the mosquito netting over her face.

She tugged at the end of her sleeves to pull them down, and all she could think about was the whine of a mosquito flying near, its tiny high-pitched hum. She became so flustered that she stuffed her hands up inside her sleeves. An emptiness engulfed her. Though the worst part, she realized, wasn't the hollow feeling of telling everything to that priest, it was the agony she felt about the vampiric nature of the world, how the very blood pumping life through her body this second could be taken from her, only to be sitting in the belly of an insect the next.

XV

ONCE AT HOME, Lila began to feel strange. She was still ruminating on all the chaos of the appointment with Dr. Peralta, of the confession. *Why did I do that?* A gnawing dread crept over her. *Because they will be here soon. Because you wanted someone to save you. But no one will save you.*

Her eyes were still puffy from crying, but she felt off, all wrong. She stared at herself in the mirror. The once-little swell had grown into a small round shelf, then a ball, and even still, she felt herself expanding. Air caught in her chest from a stabbing pain in her belly, a slurry of movement inside. She remembered the nurse telling her that stress can cause Braxton Hicks contractions, to wait it out, time it, try to relax.

"Don't panic. When the big moment comes, you'll know."

But how? How will I know?

Lila wheezed in another breath, gritting her teeth at the pain. She imagined what she would do if the swarms came now with no one around, when there was nowhere to run, no way to protect herself. She thought of the sludge from the worms, the slime in Dr. Peralta's mouth. She felt the slime making its way down her legs, a small gush of liquid. Her water broke. Taking off her pants, Lila was horrified at the physical evidence of seeing this in her underwear. She removed them, still refusing to believe it.

For months, she had ignored all the times Vivian or anyone else mentioned the forsaken words *birth plan* to her. Two words she wanted to erase out of existence, reminding her that she needed to be ready for this. Should she call Vivian? Drive herself to the hospital? Would she be safe there? She instantly had a flashback about the mud wasps at the OBGYN office and reasoned that, no, she would not be safe. *Will I be safe anywhere? What do I do?*

There wasn't even much amniotic fluid, barely enough to prove it happened. *Maybe it didn't*, she tried to convince herself.

A small moment of awareness washed over her, a knowing that she would never be the same. Like all other markers of womanhood, just one moment of many in the pattern of the body's betrayal, being sexualized as a girl for the first time, seeing the first stain of blood in your underwear, a warning of more suffering to come. The pain of penetration. And now, the burning and tearing, something wanting out. Forever a reminder that this body, the only home you'll ever have, will make you suffer. This body will cause more pain than you can possibly endure.

A radiating pain pulsed through her insides, reaching the back of her thigh, then to her hip flexor, spreading throughout her lower back. She held a hand to her back, trying to put pressure on the pain. Realizing she needed heat, to lie down, to figure out what she should do. So she went to the only safe place she could think of: the tub.

She ran a bath, eager to have warm water enveloping her, the waves of liquid like being rocked in the womb. Warmth to dull everything, even if it was slight. Even if it only lasted a minute. Anything to offset the panic, the physical agony. She undressed and gathered up some towels, decided she needed a book and maybe to drink some water.

With the tub filling, she headed back to her room for the glass of water beside her bed.

"Back labor is the worst," she remembered someone chattering on in the waiting room of one of her blurred-together appointments. "It's pure suffering. I swear to God, I thought I was going to die when I gave birth. No one ever tells you that, about all the deaths. Sometimes I'm still amazed I lived."

Lila tried to block that out now, but her body overpowered her thoughts. A surge of pain crippled her, and she gripped at the wall to steady herself. As quickly as it came, it passed.

Why is this happening so fast? This can't be right. This isn't happening.

She straightened back up, rattled, but standing. She took a few deep breaths, trying to think calm thoughts about books. About soaking in the tub. About anything that wasn't this or the return. About what it would be like to have a single second of peace, to lie in the fetal position and revert to that place of languagelessness, water covering her ears, feeling the submersion into security. When she reached for her nightstand to pick up the glass of water, her arm went slack, all strength left her, and she dropped it, spilling a puddle onto the carpet.

The agony returned, even worse than before. She buckled at the knees, no longer able to stand or hold herself up. Sliding to the floor, then padding around the carpet helplessly, she rolled onto her back and whimpered. Everything went bleary, unbearable, from a sudden violent contraction rushing in a racing crescendo of burning pain like wildfire, her cervix stretching too quickly, ripping open for birth. A howling wind rattled the window, and her eyes darted to it in a panic, scanning the skies for any signs of them.

"What does going into labor feel like?" she remembered asking the nurse at her first obstetrics appointment, the day they confirmed she was pregnant.

"Like the worst period cramps of your life," the nurse had said. "But it'll be worth it. The hardest pains bring the greatest reward."

She lied, Lila thought. *This isn't right. Something is not right.* Lila clutched her stomach as a small, labored scream erupted from her throat. *This is not like cramps. Contractions aren't supposed to feel like this. This is like something burrowing through me. This is like…* And her thoughts spun into an incoherent blur of pain signals, as if her body was shutting down, overflowing with toxins, or everything was wrong with it at once.

Lila struggled to breathe, her lungs on fire, her chest tight, heart leaping erratically to provide her body the blood it needed to keep her alive. She thought her heart might be failing, that maybe this was a heart attack. Her pain prison prevented her from moving. She wondered between teeth-clenching, wheezing breaths of agony what she would do when they came crawling one by one. Some flying, some inching, others slugging along. More liquid and mess began leaking out of her, her immense belly not getting any smaller. Lila felt the pain as if millions of wasps were stinging her, their ferocity splitting her tender, teenage skin, refusing mercy, tearing her open. She called out for her mother, but she knew that Vivian wasn't home. She was alone.

She felt the fury of them gusting around inside, urging to leave the dark place, to face the world and fight. They were swarming now, covering every inch of her.

First it was the black locusts, leaping and croaking, then the beetles slipping through and worms lolling along in time for the centipedes and millipedes' countless legs to step with hurried ferocity over undulations of skin, glistening wet from birth. The grasshoppers arrived leaping for air. The sun spiders and Goliath beetles, silverfish, hornets, and cockroaches all grouped together in unison, ribbed shells shining, scuttling with the coordination of a colony of marching ants, together like brethren, among the dobsonflies like spitting confetti darkening up the ceiling.

The room filled with a ferocious buzz, so loud that Lila covered her ears and couldn't hear her own howling screams over their flapping and whirring, shadowing her vision with black. Blood and liquids and larvae seeped from between her legs while her heartbeat raced, vicious in war.

XVI

ON THE OTHER side of the city, Nazaret was leaving the office and heading through the parking lot. She absently looked to the lined spaces of asphalt, Tesla after Mercedes after Acura after Range Rover—all the cars that belonged to the doctors and medical staff who worked in their building. An eerie stillness lingered, the trees not even stirring. It was an unusual moment of silence, no whirring of engines or cars, no one outside talking, a lull. She almost felt bad about what happened with Lila, but she didn't take responsibility for her clients' feelings.

She shoved her blood-spotted hand into her bag for her car keys, and when she pulled them out, a fly landed on her wrist. Waving her arm to shoo it, she looked down to find two more had landed where the first one had been.

"Ugh!" she spat and flicked her hand in disgust, swatting at the air with more force. Repulsed, she shook out her arm, afraid to look down. *Where are they coming from? Why are there so many of them?* When she mustered the courage to look again, she exhaled in relief to find they were gone.

Even though they had flown away, she could still hear them. That sound made her on edge, angry. She finally started to understand, despite all she'd been experiencing, the chaos Lila must feel constantly. The way that sound could make someone lose it.

Is one still on me?

She swatted around her, and to be safe, moved her hair to one shoulder, then ran her fingers through the ends. It didn't help. She could still hear it. *Did one fly into my hair? Why is it so loud?*

She checked the front of her shirt and shook the fabric a few times, shaking her sleeves and hair again, paranoid that maybe one flew into her bra, or worse, was creeping down her navel and into her pants. But this thought was drifting into a panic territory that she knew she had to steer away from. *Sounds like something Lila would say.* She couldn't keep getting like this, absorbing the fears of her clients. She untucked her shirt and examined it again, making certain there was nothing crawling on her or trapped in the fabric. Still, the buzzing persisted.

Frustrated, she pressed at her humming ear and pushed a finger to her tragus. It tickled as if an earwig were crawling inside her ear canal. *Oh God, is it inside of my ear?* Her hand trembled into a cupped shape, that sound rushing inside her palm. She stood completely still.

Holding her breath to listen, she realized it wasn't coming from somewhere on her, or near her, or from inside of her. It was farther away.

She turned her head up to the sky.

As if time slowed, everything suddenly quieted, the buzzing dissipated. What looked like a flock of colorful birds came flying toward her. Once they got closer, their shapes brightened. Butterflies. Tons of them.

A kaleidoscope of butterflies flooded the horizon, adorning the sky with the most luminous colors Nazaret had ever seen, vivid hues that made her whole life feel grayscale.

In awe of them, she didn't react much when she felt something land on her, something heavier than just a fly. She looked down.

A giant moth had landed on her wrist, its wingspan at least seven inches across, covering her entire hand. Despite being momentarily shocked, she wasn't disturbed by it. She'd never seen a moth in the middle of the day.

She'd also never seen one this big. Never in the sun. She thought of what Lila had told her the day they met, her fear of the moth in her office. Racking her brain for what this moth was called, its beauty enchanted her. *Emperor moth? Polyphemus moth?* Despite Lila's warnings, she didn't feel afraid of it.

The two vibrant eyespots on the back of its wings were looking at her, into her. They were outlined by dark edges, with canary yellow irises and dark dots for pupils. The rest of its body was a sandy tan, its antennae and head a beige white. Delicate, feathery wings brushed against her skin, lightly flapping every few seconds. The wings were iridescent, as though covered in glitter, angelic dust, something to flaunt to a beholder its power, to catch attention in the light. They resembled textured leaves, a perfect plant-like chameleon, but not those eyes. Those eyespots on the back of its wings almost appeared human. Godlike.

For a moment, Nazaret felt the presence of divinity, of belonging, seeing herself in all living beings and realizing the diminutiveness of her existence alongside this creature who was free enough to fly. Like staring out at the endlessness of the ocean, or the vastness of starlight. Looking into those eyespots, she felt small.

Overcome with emotion, she asked it in a soft whisper, "What are you doing here?"

It moved its wings slightly, antennae twitching.

She wondered if this was an angel, some deity coming to witness her, watch over her, or perhaps the opposite—allowing her to witness it. As it rested, she had a sinking awareness that she would never see a moth like this again.

After allowing her to behold it, the moth took flight.

She held her gaze on it until the eyespots were blurred, whispering a small prayer to them, like looking to the eyes of God. She didn't want it to leave.

A sudden piercing struck her hand. A raindrop landed with a ferocity that almost felt sharp, like a sting. Then another. Now came a pattering against the asphalt, a drizzling.

The giant moth's flight pattern became dumb and dizzied in the rain, swooping and straining against the wind. Haziness loomed over the shifting sky, now almost glowing. It was so suddenly magnificent that she couldn't believe it was real. There was a new brightness, vibrant and fiery, radiating the warmth of a sunset, the horizon rich with yellow and orange.

She felt as if she was now trapped in amber, fossilized in place, observing a new, terrifying world. The sky started to simmer, shifting in its impermanence, glinting like a mirage. A glowing that resembled shooting stars. Then the tiny falling stars faded and fell, their light simmering out. As they got closer, she realized these stars were aflame.

A grayish haze coated the horizon, as if the leaves on the nearby trees seemed to be covered in frost, which didn't make sense in the heat. Nazaret had only seen snow a few times in her life, never here. As the stars got closer, a burning smell emerged, sending her into a sudden coughing fit. The thick fog engulfing her became a cloud of ash.

The famous Robert Frost poem came to her mind, musing on the end of the world. She had never fully understood that poem before, but here and now, underneath this sky, she did. *What is that?* She stared at the sky. *Are those falling stars? Are those…bats?*

Winged creatures fluttered toward her, flapping frantically, struggling to fly through the weather. As they emerged into view, moths flitted past her, alight with fire, dropping from the sky. Clusters of them rushed toward her in a frenzy, some falling over her head. The moths were whirring and fluttering in frantic patterns of flight, attracted to the burn in each other, crashing into one another, igniting each other further.

Their embers contrasted against the murky sky. The gray backlit a dull orange, like the gleam of the horizon was tilted, closing in on her, trapping her in a feeling of both uncertain impermanence and imprisonment.

Staring at the flickers in the haze, she felt weak, unsteady, the way she did in the searing heat of summer. Light speckled across the horizon like the whisper of gleaming stars over the dark graveyard where she'd prayed for her tata on the day he died, the last time she could remember praying.

The land transformed into some glowing amber hellscape. The moth's fiery corpses were still raining down from above, with more pouring in over the blighted skyline. Nazaret shielded her eyes, covering her face, feeling their bodies flutter against her, suddenly afraid the singes might catch and ignite in her hair. Despite getting drizzled on, her clothes were mostly dry. The little moments of impact burned her skin, and she couldn't differentiate between raindrops and the hot touch of their wings. Fear welled inside of her, surrounded by stinging rain and the fallout of dying moths engulfed in flames.

The buzzing returned to her full force. The growing hum became a low roar, a hard growl, arriving louder and more persistent, just over the horizon. When she squinted, she saw the sky grouping together, overtaken by an immense dark cloud.

"Holy shit," she said quietly, remembering the storm warnings battering through the news cycle all day, the emergency broadcast on the radio in the car that morning, the earsplitting beep crackling through the speakers.

SEVERE THUNDERSTORM WARNING WITH FLASH FLOOD WARNING IS REPORTED FOR THE FOLLOWING COUNTIES:

She had shut the radio off without listening and thought now of Gabe's concerned texts: "Try to get home before the storm. I don't want you driving in hail or a flood or whatever is supposed to hit tonight." Later, he tried with: "Nazaret?" And then a call she didn't answer, followed by another text with twelve question marks. Then there were the multiple assaults from her phone blaring emergency alerts. Her last client even canceled, not wanting to risk this weather.

She stood paralyzed in a strange frozen awe, watching the blackness spread across the sky. It was mesmerizing, beautiful. A promise of deliverance—the noise blaring as the dark descended.

Before she could blink, they were upon her, a flurry of swarming insects, masses of them cloaking the landscape in a sharp buzz, making hard clattering landings against the metal surfaces of cars, shattering glass windows, dents forming all along the corner mailboxes while their slamming into rocks made impact like thunderous war drums. The cloud grew, coating the street in convoluted black. Antennae, wings, and multi-eyed faces covered her body in a whirl, so thick she couldn't see—everything gone dark and covered up until there was nothing left, only the sounds of invasion.

SHORT FICTION

JUST US

I GO TO see Renaldo again in the cemetery, and even after visiting so many times, I still get lost. Aimlessly, I walk, circling the same never-ending stretch of graves, not caring that I'm trampling over resting places for the hordes of dead. Time is leaving me. I'm back in my body, my left foot, my right. Renaldo, where are you? I call out to him between sobs, panicking that maybe he really is gone forever.

Finally, my feet bring me to his headstone, and I glance at the dirt in piles next to an unholy empty spot in the ground. His grave has been disturbed. A groundskeeper with the deepest smoker's voice I've ever heard is shouting at me, saying something about the corpse. It's all crazy-speak, that someone's dragged Renaldo as far as the east gate with the angel mausoleum. I don't want to see, but I run over to the mausoleum anyway.

It's only been a few months since he died, so he's not fully decomposed. Renaldo already looks like another person, like something else. Still, I'm surprised to realize that the exhumed burial plot is worse. His empty grave haunts me more than his body strewn haphazardly in the wrong place on the cemetery lawn. That unearthed pit in the ground suggests that maybe he was never here, like he's already moved on, gone to another place.

And then there's me, left behind.

Since Renaldo died I haven't known what to do with myself, how to exist anymore. At first, people said they were sorry, that they wanted to be there for me, but that was a lie. After their one attempt at faking they cared, they never called. Never asked a single question, like his death was the most boring event they'd ever been forced to endure. Worse, they made sure to never bring up Renaldo again. Everything went on as if this was one bad day, like my whole life didn't just end, like Renaldo was dead all along. Like he never existed. And what a terrible thing to do to a grieving person, to their dead. To be so indifferent, so cruel.

I once heard that a person dies two deaths, first when they pass, and again when their name is uttered for the very last time. It's like everyone just wants the dead to stay dead, for them to rot in the ground and silence anyone who knew them too. But I'll never stop speaking of Renaldo. Even if no one will listen. He always listened to me. *Listened*, like it's all over, like *we're over*, but I'm not so convinced.

After the shock of everything at the cemetery, I realize I need a way to reach him, for us to talk. I still don't know if he hears me. Do you hear me, Renaldo? Are you there?

I find a few psychics online but turns out they are all frauds preying on grief and heartache and desperation. One looks me dead in the eyes and lies, says *Your loved one has moved on to the other side. They are at peace now.* Only that's not true. None of this is peace.

Another psychic calls herself a medium and tells me she can converse with anyone beyond the grave. She holds my hands over a table adorned with purple velvet, jasmine incense burning fragrantly in the corner of her small storefront. There's candles and tarot cards and piles of crystals everywhere. We close our eyes. She says she's summoned him, but I think she just invited whoever would come. Whoever it is, it's not Renaldo. I know it isn't.

Because she shudders like something's wrong, then she opens her eyes to look at me, and with a disgusted look on her face she says, "Get out."

Without protest, I leave, though I don't give up. I try virtual sessions with more mediums, but each time it's like they invent a dead person from scratch, someone totally made up. They say things about peace, letting go, more bullshit. That's not Renaldo. Renaldo is darkness. Renaldo is truth. Renaldo would say he hates this, that these people are all liars. He would say that Mason has to pay for what he's done.

Anyway, I don't want to do this anymore, stuck in-between, doomed to rely on other people who only let me down. Eventually I surrender to the fact that I have to find a way to speak to him on my own.

Renaldo? I ask. Where are you, Renaldo?

I try to picture his face, to never lose it. It happens to the dead, they just fade away. I won't let it happen to Renaldo. I want to remember everything. Every little damn thing. Even that disgusting cherry balm he would always glob on so thick I could see little chunks of wax or lanolin or whatever it is from animals they torture to turn into ChapStick. The glistening sheen on his stubble above his Cupid's bow always repulsed me.

And then there's his scar. Your scar looks like you were dragged by a fishhook, curling over your lip like an invisible thread, I say to him out loud.

Not many people would notice it. But I was there when it happened. I think I was, right? I ask him. I must have been. I remember when you fell off the ladder of the diving board, my world going black when your head slammed against the pool deck. Even now, I can almost taste that coppery wound in my mouth. You lost a tooth. I'd never been more afraid, but you pulled through. Not like this time. Not after what Mason did.

The last time I saw you, you were wearing your U of A sweatshirt, ARIZONA printed in red across the front. I remember when your face hit the asphalt, Mason stomping the back of your skull, some men running over to pull him off of you. I remember when they turned you over and you had little rocks in your face and bloody dirt packed into your split open head. I remember screaming, someone's arms pulling me back, everything going foggy until I woke up and they told me it was all real, that you were dead.

Images come back to me, the way your puffed-up eye barely opened, how you looked at me one last time before they took you away. Our last moment together when you were alive.

But we can still be together, Renaldo.

Here I am, walking and talking for hours, and I'll walk all night, through morning, who knows? My feet are forever bringing me back to the only place I know to go.

Now you're here. In Grace Lily Cemetery, plot 4G9. I let my eyes span my surroundings across the landscape of graves, take in the scenery, and turn to the lettering that reads *Renaldo Ortiz* engraved in stone.

Look at all these people, Renaldo, I say as I stare back out at the rows of gray headstones. Look at these people who have no one. All these people who are forgotten. Not you. I don't know how many days it's been. How many times I've come here, sat on the grass, picked at flower petals, read your name. Tried to guess where I end and you begin. Whenever I come to pass the hours with you, I fall asleep on the grass and wake to the groundskeeper chasing me out. I don't understand why I can't sleep here. People mourn at night. At night's when everything's worse.

Here we lie, Renaldo. You and I, us, forever together. I burrow my hand through the grass, claw up some of your grave dirt. I put it in a baggie so I can keep it. Have the earth that holds you. Each time I dig a little deeper, get as close to you as I can.

Soon the groundskeeper will come after me again, trying to keep us apart. Your dirt is important to me, so we can remember this part of our story. We'll laugh about this, one day. All you have to do is come back.

Just come back.

AFTER RENALDO'S FUNERAL, his abuela called me and invited me to pick up some of his things. She sobbed and I hugged her tight, the saddest hug. We sat for a while at the table, the clock ticking on the wall marking the slow passage of time like some horrible wail. We looked at a few of his baby pictures. Cried into our coffee. At Abuela's, I took home some of Renaldo's drawings, a few pages of his journals. Things to keep him near.

When I think about it, I realize I was never a whole person until we met. Then he was murdered and something's missing again, I'm no longer me. So I bundled up all of Renaldo's shirts and piled them in bed, made them into the shape of him. That way he's with me, even when I can't be with him in the cemetery. It took a lot of work to acquire this, but I start wearing that U of A sweatshirt. The one he died in.

Don't you know that, Renaldo? How desperately I need you? Don't you understand this pain I'm in?

I know he must hear me. When he's ready, he'll talk back. All I have to do is listen.

At last, I finally hear him. First it's his breath, then I hear him say my name, almost like it's inside my head, already in my ears, his voice part of me as if it were uttered from my own lips.

In bed, bundled up next to the shirt-lumps of Renaldo, I lie still, breathing in his smell. Listening. Holding my breath. Waiting for him to breathe back. To say something again, anything.

What's that, Renaldo? Did you say something?

He tells me he misses me, but not really, because he isn't gone. And you can't miss someone who isn't gone.

Then he says, *I want to wear your skin.*

I smile. No, I want to wear *your* skin, I say, and we go back and forth in this way, swapping skins. I crawl out of bed, run my fingertips along my body, feel its strange texture. I'm standing in front of the mirror, examining myself. Now I'm imitating his voice, his sway, his facial expressions. Scrunching up my eyebrows in surprise, like Renaldo.

I roll up my sleeves and hold up my arm to the glass, unshaven with visible dark hair. Like his. My skin is a strange foreign phenomenon, some suit sagged over me.

I even smell like you, I tell him. I have a new taste for black coffee, how you like it. It's all I'll drink now. I wonder if anyone notices. Of course they don't. No one notices a thing. But I do, Renaldo. I always have. I know all the things you love, hold all the pieces of you.

There's so much to tell him. So much to catch up on.

. You know what else? Speaking of, I tried to go for coffee with that bitch you never liked, Monica, my old friend from college, you remember? My first attempt at being human after you were buried and dug back up. And you know what she said to me? Nothing. She looked at your sweatshirt—our sweatshirt—didn't even mention you. Didn't utter your name. Kept looking down every five seconds and clacking her fake fingernails against the glass on her phone, smiling at it, like there was something in this fucked-up world to smile about.

Then I heard a barista call out the name Renaldo, and I turned, nearly leapt from my seat. Monica finally lifted her head to look at me, she goes, "Are you okay?" And I could just hear the disdain in her voice, the embarrassment. I tried to tell her that it was proof you were here with us, with me. But she didn't listen. Her phone rang, and she held up a finger and said, "Hang on, hold that thought," answered it right in the middle of me speaking. About you.

It's horrible to share something so personal—so painful— to someone who doesn't care. It's worse than saying nothing at all. So we won't tell anymore. We don't need to. It's better if no one knows a thing. Our little secret, Renaldo. Just us.

You know something else, Renaldo? I say. This might be more than hearing you. I've been thinking a lot about reincarnation, like maybe when you die, you really do become someone else, born the second you're gone. But do you start over? Or just get inserted? I saw this documentary about kids with weird memories. Memories impossible to have. Some six-year-old who knows how to fly a freight hangar from the thirties, another kid that knows crew members' names from the Titanic, including the exact location of all the tables before they turned into floating splinters. There was even a little girl pointing to where Anne Frank cut out pictures and hung them on walls. Things no one could teach.

I mean, does the soul always jump into a newborn? Or can it go to an already occupied body?

Oh, Renaldo. Am I you? Are you me? Are we really one? Where are we, Renaldo? How did we get here?

At night I dream of the fight with Mason. And I see it through your eyes. I feel the blood coursing in your head. In mine. I see the slip off the diving board, feel that sink in my gut from the fall. I feel the blackout of impact, the slash of broken skin, that scar burning my lip.

Do you think we're someone new, something else? Or still us? Are you there, Renaldo? I wrap my arms around myself, breathe in deeply. Yes. You're here. It's you and me. Like always. We can't ever be apart. Not truly.

Anyway, that bitch Monica finally calls me up, and I answer it. She asks me what the hell my problem was the other day, if something happened at Renaldo's grave. That I looked dirty and reeked of death, that at first she thought it was some grunge thing I was going for—and I cut her off, say that we always hated her, that she knows nothing about us. She hung up, but she's only pissed I wasn't fanning her ego, making it all about her.

You know who isn't a horrible bitch though, Renaldo? Abuela. I wanted to do something nice for her, so I wrote her a little something. Sent her the handwritten note with a Polaroid of us smiling, wearing the sweatshirt, and signed it *Renaldo*. I know it will make her happy. I told her we are coming by soon. Do you think it's okay to show up unannounced? It took me a while to realize that you're here, and I want her to be surprised. I took some of the grave dirt, sprinkled a little in the envelope. She'll love it, I just know.

I can't wait to tell her. To tell everyone. To show them. To leave these months of agony behind. To bask in the warmth of you here with me, to feel your flesh on mine, to do everything we've always wanted.

I take our index finger and drag it across the mirror, touch at the place where our hairline reflects back at us. Your black eyes in mine. Our dark hair. Our tan skin. Your lisp coming out of my mouth. My teeth a little more crooked, our scar clearly visible now.

For a moment, I'm startled by this, seeing you here, really seeing you, but I just listen to your breath exhaling out of my lungs. Watch your long eyelashes batting across my eyelids. I look at the reflection: greasy hair, arm trembling from holding up my finger against the glass for so long. I can't remember the last time I've slept. Has my hair always been this thin? Why does it look like I'm going bald? Like you, Renaldo? All my hair that's been falling out is gathering in a little nest on my lap. I can see that cowlick from the edge of your hairline, now creeping up over my widow's peak, almost receding. There's grave dirt all over our sweatshirt. This sweatshirt that isn't coming off.

Where are you, Renaldo? Are you here?

I stare for a long while, plant my lips on the mirror to kiss you. I can see you, looking back at me, and I'm absolutely certain, at last, I know where you are. It has all been so funny, hasn't it? Together we realize this and start to laugh.

I dig in our pocket, pull out your favorite ChapStick, *our* favorite. I'm coating the hell out of our lips with this cherry balm, and it tastes good.

MY OTHER HALF

Originally Published in *Dark Matter Magazine*

I JOINED THE new dating service Together Again, and I'll admit it's a little extreme, but I can't bring myself to try anything else because I've had too many terrible relationships. When you're a giver, you just end up with takers. My major issue is that I only seem to encounter two types of men: sweet, normal ones who are afraid of me, who would never approach me and who can't string two words together if I speak to them; or the abusive ones who lead with charm and lies and narcissistic mirroring on their way to trapping me into an eventual terror-stricken existence while they slowly exert more control until I'm a prisoner stuck in a dark pit for years that almost becomes my grave, grasping at my calculated plans of escape and strategizing daily how I'm going to stay alive. So, I don't know how to meet people. How else am I supposed to find you?

The cost is astronomical, but what about the cost of *not* finding you? That's not something I can risk anymore. I haven't been a member that long, but long enough to convince me you're here. It's how they have so many users. The efficiency. The hope. I'm meeting dates outside of my normal two shitty categories. I'm having fun. Which to be honest, I don't care about. All I care about is you.

What sold me is the safety angle. I don't have to worry about getting murdered or worse by some psycho. There's zero chance of pregnancy. No sexual risks. No social repercussions. All this to say, a lot of people join this place. Most are desperate to find their other halves, though many of us are consoled by limitless sex with strangers. That alone is worth the money.

The facility is pristine, but nightmarish. Like a haunted brothel meets a hospital. I check in and put on the issued contact lenses. These lenses initiate a virtual reality blended with physical experience—you feel everything. You're not trapped in a booth or strapped into a headset. It's all structured like a game, probably to help everyone take it lightly since lonely people get sad when they don't find their half. Whenever a match generates, they're rendered as an incredibly lifelike 3D printing of their body. You can touch them and interact with the avatars as if it's the actual person, who is also having the same real-time interaction with your avatar from wherever they are. The technology is highly advanced, it's almost impossible to tell it's not real. I don't understand how it works. I just pay the fee.

Together again, at last. That's glowing on an e-banner in the lobby. I get in line with the other users. The premise is they're reconstructing you, making you whole. Finding your missing soulmate torn away by Zeus back when humans were still paired with two heads, four arms, and four legs. It's not just a marketing thing. These people really believe in this. We all do. There's a team of doctors studying it. They are always watching, peering down at us from a second-floor lab room behind some creepy two-way mirror.

Another weird thing is that ever since I joined, I've been having this dream. You and I are holding hands on a beach. We're getting stitched together by some cloaked deity. Its skeletal hand is wielding an enormous, curved needle. You're crying, and I can't see your face so I don't know what you look like, but I'm holding you, telling you that it's all going to be okay. The pain will leave, I say. Everything you went through is over. Everything from before has led us here, to this moment. After all this time, we found each other. And I know it sounds crazy, but that's how I know am going to meet you soon.

The settings are limited, just sexuality preferences. Zeus scattered halves across the Earth, so you might match with someone at a Together Again facility in another country or they could be someone in a processing room ten feet away from you. Matches are mostly random. Same as in real life, you don't have control over who you meet. Muting sex is also an option, so if you don't want it, it won't give you people who do. I never, ever pick that. That is the opposite of what I want. I can't imagine going through all of this, not finding my half, and then not even getting consequences-free fucked.

The fact that I got myself ready and walked into this place is miraculous. I could never do dating like this in real life. I can't even go to the grocery store unless I hide weapons on myself in case a man tries to abduct me, or in case one of my stalkers finds me, or in case it's another man who wants to hurt me. It's always a new face but the same man.

I've learned that I must constantly expect to have to fight for my life, and whenever a man oversteps a line I oscillate between being a snarling aggressive bitch or a dissociated rock but nothing ever works to keep me safe. It just becomes so much stress that I can't leave the house, where even there I fear men will find me. No amount of big dogs or guns or therapy can help me, because I know too well that while there are beautiful people in this world, all it takes is one bad man to destroy you. So I guess it's nice coming here, because here I don't have to be afraid. Unlike on a real date, none of these men can hurt me.

The fee buys an hour, and you can skip as many modes or matches as you want, but if you haven't found your half before the time is up, whoever you're with when the timer strikes 00:00 is who you're stuck with and you get fused. The process is instantaneous, done by some robotic surgery. If they're not your half, you go to the cut floor to suffer through a severing then wait out the healing to come back and try again, hoping your true half won't mind all the wounds.

Their business model is working because I'm here all the time now. I just signed onto an auto-pay plan. I don't even know if I can afford this. Goodbye, savings. It'll be worth it, I keep telling myself.

I'm just glad I don't have to survive a drink with someone new turning into me being held hostage and assaulted. Or an awful night with a man I think I can maybe-almost-hopefully start to trust, only to later learn he's put tracking devices in my vehicle, stalked me via social media so I have to delete it forever, and he now waits for me in the parking lot at my work with flowers. He's luring me inside his car, pretending he's reserved a surprise for our fifth date but really he's driving me out to the middle of the desert until we run out of gas. I have no idea where we are and he's distraught and waving a pistol around in my face for six and a half hours, snatching my phone from my trembling hands so I can't call 911, and he's telling me I can't leave him, that I better answer the fucking phone when he calls, that I belong with him, that he loves me.

Then I'm years deep in this and now it's a different man and a different weapon but my entire life is the exact same day on repeat. He's always keeping my phone so I can't call for help, and my keys so I can't go anywhere. One morning he takes my shoes so I can't try to run while he's in a full rage and I still make it through the front door but he catches up to me at the car. I'm forever trapped in this car. It's in these moments of failure that I'm reminded I'm alone. It's not like I have anyone to call or anywhere to go. Even if this is some miracle like in the movies where I can just make unmonitored calls to anyone I want, or go places without him, or somehow get out of this vehicle without getting shot, who are they going to believe? Me, with zero evidence, or a veteran with no criminal history who's got jokes and perfect ass-kissing composure? Even if a domestic disturbance gets documented, even if he's arrested—which won't happen—the instant he's out on bail, guess who's going to get a fist to the ribs or a bullet in the stomach for being a lying whore who fell down the stairs? And this time if I say anything, he's going to kill my dog.

For a while he'll be nice, and I'll be so relieved and delusional, I'll think it's finally over. But it's never over. Time is sinking into a vacuum. It's all one bleary stretch of the same identical haze of treading for air in a state of no-sleep adrenaline. When you have no family and all you've got is a job and a place to live and nowhere else to go and no money to go anywhere anyway, slipping off your modest cliff is a long way down. Then there's always the gut-sink reminder that even if you were homeless, he'd find you.

I used to think that maybe this is all there is for me. Maybe I should just be grateful to be alive. That my face isn't black and blue, that so many people have it worse. Who am I to want a better life? Who am I to want anything? Maybe it's okay if he kills me. But then I would tell myself I can't die, I have to protect this dog. The dog and I have to make it. And we do. Because of this dog, I am breathing.

There aren't risks like that here. I don't have to fear that anymore. That isn't my life anymore. That will never be my life again.

All of this is safe. There's a panic setting if something goes wrong. Predators aren't an issue because they can't pass the pre-screenings. It's strict. People get banned for the tiniest infractions. You never get matched to the same person twice, so it's impossible to be stalked, and that way there's a higher chance of finding your half in the sea of people. It's a good system. Because if you meet your half, you'll know. It's not something you need to experience twice to figure out. If you have to even think about it, you haven't met them yet.

The last time I was in here was two weeks ago, and my final match obviously wasn't my half. I knew we had to separate even though it was regrettable, because he was super hot. It was GAME OVER and he was fused to me, then we were sliced in half on the cut floor, blood spouting everywhere. You can choose laser cauterization or a gore fest. We both liked the gore, so that's what we got. *Mortal Kombat* fans understand. Even in this nightmare, this sick bloodbath, him covered in red, I still wanted him. I wanted to smear the blood all over me and I wanted him to lick it off of my body. I wanted him to lap it up the way I want to suck Billy Loomis's fingers in the original *Scream.*

What does that say about me? That I want to fuck Billy senseless, that having this serial killer's blood-slathered fingers inside me is all I can picture when I see that reveal scene. That this consumes me until my thoughts are only random flashes of feral filth where I'm Billy Loomis's final girl.

I'm seeing red. The red rotation light is flickering along the walls. Finally, there's the bell. Time for a rotation. Even if you don't skip a match, the rotations move the line along. The doors are changing, randomly assigning.

My door opens and I get a double. Sometimes they do this, a bonus perk. These two in front of me are definitely himbos. They look like carbon copies of each other, and a little like Michael B. Jordan. Identical twins. Lucky me. Every time I see twins, I have this problem about imagining them being my lovesick Romeos.

So I'm their dream woman, both of them, and they're competing for me. They are extra well-behaved with perfect manners, showering me in love and affection, stupid-expensive gifts, constant worship, but neither ever wins me over. They can't quite figure out what I want, but they don't give up. Between the full-body massages, breakfast in bed, my every wish as their command, they try everything they can think of to spoil me, each hoping they're the one I'll finally choose. Only I keep telling them I haven't made up my mind yet and they keep working harder to please me. And so it goes, this never-ending double-vision of washboard abs and hands that can do no wrong, hands that would never hurt me, hands that…

Now I'm back to Billy Loomis's bloody hands again, and my clitoris has its own pulse. Gods, if you're real, please let it be Billy when they open my next door. These twin himbos unfortunately aren't mine. I just want my half. Or Billy. I press the button to skip.

Oh great, it's lagging. The himbos are buffering.

There's another match delay, so they set me up to play FMK. Everyone knows this game: Fuck, Marry, Kill. When this place overflows with users, they throw you into free bonus rounds while they configure matches. They don't pair you with real users for FMK, which they say would be cruel. I think it would be fun. Instead, they pair you with famous people. You can pick categories: musicians, actors, painters, athletes, whatever. I pick writers.

It's loading.

My matches are Ernest Hemingway, F. Scott Fitzgerald, and Edgar Allan Poe. A combination I don't even have to think about.

Immediately, I am excited to kill Ernest. I get to choose between a chainsaw, a Tommy gun, and a meat cleaver. I pick up the cleaver and start hacking. His blood splatters all over me. We're making an enormous mess. I wish they would add in some *Mortal Kombat* style fatalities for this mode because I would love to thrust Scorpion's spear through Ernest's skull, then reel him in on that chain, and do it again up close.

For the "Fucking" portion, you just get a bed. They do try to recreate how the person would behave. My bed has F. Scott in it. Our night together is tender, and he is a decent lover. He cries after sex, which I should have guessed would happen, but it's still jarring for me and I have to try not to laugh, not because men crying is funny, it's not. But because it's F. Scott Fitzgerald and I can just imagine him leaving Zelda in an asylum to die while he steals her writing and claims it as his own, then sobs through sleeping with random women. I realize I find him pathetic. It makes sense that he and Hemingway were close.

Then there's Edgar, my dream man. I am dolled up and waiting to marry him in a graveyard. I want him to rip my heart from my chest or put me under some floorboards. I am ready to consummate this union. I'll do anything he says. Anything, Edgar.

His family hasn't shown up, I think because they're dead, and his army buddies are obliterated on absinthe. One might even be a ghost because he has a hell of a lot of shrapnel smattered all along his face. Another has trench foot so bad that someone has to wheel him through the aisles. I don't like the parasol that goes with my bridal corset. This outfit is paralyzing and I can barely move. What I really want is to take all of this shit off and throw my arms around Edgar and gaze into his black eyes. I want to ask him to write me poems. To read me poems. To write about me. To just let me look at him. To just stand there and be perfect.

I'm still lost in a love-struck daze staring at him when our time together vanishes. I don't even get to kiss him. And here I am, back in the roster queue for the next round. Among the other hopefuls, waiting for you.

A new mode is starting: Seven Minutes in Heaven. Most people use this one for sex, because they just throw you in a dark closet with someone, but you never know. Love is in the air. It will find you where you least expect.

I don't know what I would do if I met you in Heaven. What are we supposed to tell our grandchildren when they ask? That we really paid for this? That we fell in love while groping each other in a closet? It's pitch-black in here. What if they ask if it was love at first sight? With someone as special as you, of course it is.

Whoever is in here with me starts kissing me. Then I think about what it will be like when you kiss me. I dream all the time about kissing you, about the coyness in your voice when you're trying to hide your want, how it'll feel with my hips to your hips, ribs to ribs, lips touching yours. There's something so spiritual about our deep, nirvana-kissing, the kind that would just be revolting with anyone else.

But with you? You could lick honey out of my mouth, sensual and slow, until the desire becomes a force, your kiss pushing harder against mine, teeth hitting teeth, lips going numb, you telling me everything you're thinking without words. Our own little language. It's how you know exactly what I'm saying without me having to say it, and anyone else would never understand.

This nobody is pulling me onto his lap, but it's okay, I'm still imagining it's you. Now the rest of you has risen to life. I can feel the music of your heart. Your hands are gripping my waist, ever the gentleman, not yet straying to more enticing places—pulling me to your erection pressing against me, pleading to be known. In time, love. We will have an eternity of knowing.

There's the bell. The red light is glittering across my match's eyes. He looks delirious with lust. I stumble out through the door and find my place back in the rotation pool. I don't even remember anything about that nobody in there. All I know is he wasn't you. I should have skipped him immediately, but I get too in my head when I'm thinking of you. I always forget to remind myself how much I hate this mode, that I don't want to do Heaven anymore.

What I really want to be doing right now is moaning your name. What *is* your name? Why can't I at least know that? Where the hell are you? Why haven't I found you yet?

I switch back to regular dates. My next room opens. Is this some glitch? I'm looking at the most gorgeous woman I've ever seen. I chose men for my preferred gender, because I'm ninety-nine percent sure my half is a man, but who can remember their blurry sexuality when she looks like that? One of the gods or the algorithm must be testing me.

She's wearing blood-red lipstick and her perfect cleavage is threatening to escape her crop top, a focal point demanding attention. Her necklace holds a pendant or something. A cross? A heart? I don't want to stare, but whatever it is has been swallowed into her tits. I'm too nervous to talk. She greets me and says something but my head is cotton. Hi, I say back, stupidly, and we hug. The sexual tension is suffocating, for me at least. She smells like an angel, like Marc Jacobs Dot, or maybe Daisy. Those perfumes smell the same to me. She's ethereal. I think I understand what these men feel when they are giving me the deer-in-headlights face. A crippling paralysis is now seizing every inch of me.

I can't deal with her outfit. Her nipple barbells are showing through her tiny shirt and I'm glad that mine aren't pierced anymore so we won't get them caught when I desperately hope this ends with more than a conversation. I'll die if they fuse us and then cut us in half because there's no way I'm going to skip her, and this one's a loss that's going to hurt.

This stunned idiocy I'm experiencing reminds me of a few weeks ago when I almost had sex with some guy in the last round. I wasn't really that into him, it's just that everyone gets impulsive in the final minutes, but it didn't end up happening because I accidentally overwhelmed him.

I wasn't even touching him yet and was still working on his belt when I playfully told him that he was not allowed to come. Playful was how I meant it, even though I realize my sexual presence is not exactly playful so maybe this was my fault when it had the opposite effect. He reacted as though I gave him some kind of command, like this was something I was going to be able to actually enforce, and he liked it a little too much. I thought he was going to ejaculate with his pants still on when I started to kiss his throat. Then he definitely did, and I didn't care about that and tried to reassure him that it was okay but he went into a shame spiral, so I must have embarrassed him more because he put his head in his hands and it was like I suddenly didn't exist. The same familiar sting as always, when men are finished and that means I am dissipated into the fucking air or something and now their work is done here.

I didn't have to do anything, which I guess made it easy. Though it's no fun if your plaything is already tapped out of the game in the same time it takes you to straddle him and whisper in his ear. That's not my half. My half wants to play cat and mouse for eternity, understands our catharsis is endless. How feeling unbridled is an intoxicating thing. My half can conjure desire with one look and make it last years, following me around like a ghost.

Now she's making jokes. She's funny. I'm laughing. I love her lipstick. I want her to leave lip prints all over my thighs. I'm amazed she still hasn't skipped me. Her skirt is cute. I need one for myself. Her nails are pretty. Should I try to hold her hand? No, that's stupid. Why is this so terrifying? I'm just not going to move. I'm going to sit here like a brick and wait for breath to enter and exit my lungs.

She looks upset about something now. She's not talking anymore. She's just staring at me. Waiting for me to contribute. Shit. She's over this, over me. I still can't talk.

And I can't even hear the silence because there's this never ceasing noise from my tormented past ringing in my head, fueling my desire to skip straight to some kind of intimacy because who knows when we're going to die? People die every day. All we have is here and now and we might as well be living like it. Plus this is a beautiful woman, so of course I'm ignoring anything that could go wrong. Only in this instance, I'm what could go wrong. It's me who's got all these issues. She can see it, she's smart.

She's sizing me up. Not in a sexy way, it's in an *are you okay?* way, already knowing she'll have to be the one to end this so that I won't obsess and fall in love. She wants someone lighthearted and fun, someone who is the things I can only pretend to be for ten minutes at a time, forever regressing to this haunted, freak of a person who needs too much and gives too much and thinks love is the last chance at surviving the never-ending horrors of existence. I would only be a burden to her, and what is that? Of course, the bell. Blaring and spilling red all over the room. Casting a rose-tinted glow over her pretty face, that cleavage I'll never see again.

But neither of us gets up, which is in violation of rule number one, ignoring rotation. I'm beside myself when she slides over to me and sticks my hand up her skirt. Now my brain has skipped to the part where the skirt's already off, and that torture device of a shirt is finally off, and her lipstick tastes like vanilla, and we're touching each other.

Any minute now I'll get removed. The moderators are about to pound on the door and ban me for refusing rotation, but in all reality she's looking at me strangely, because this is a fantasy, and I need to come back to the truth that I'll never have her. That this isn't real. Nothing is real.

I can't do this anymore. I have to get out of here. Why do I keep coming back to this place? Oh, that's right. For you. I'm looking for you. I'm still, always and forever, looking for you. There are so many distractions. I keep getting lost on the path to you.

The last mode that everyone gets when there's less than fifteen minutes remaining is the Hall of Doors. I'm running out of time, and I'm so tired of this. I'm freaking out, trying not to think about the inevitable pain of when this is all over soon, having to fuse and then immediately sever with someone I don't even want, having to live another day without you. So here I am, opening doors left and right, hating myself for trying to fill the cavern-sized hole in my heart by stuffing it with whoever—anyone who wants to fill me up. None of these people are you and I don't know what I'm supposed to do anymore. The tiny glimmer of hope inside of me is dying, and now there's only a few minutes left. My fear is becoming a roar. I'm flashing back to everything I've lived through, stunned that I am still standing, that I am even still on this planet, and I didn't expect to make it this far so now I don't know where to go. I'm in constant terror that horrible things will just keep happening to me. That maybe this is doomed to be my entire life, and I'm at the mercy of my fate and forever trying to outrun it. That maybe I'm too late, that I missed you, and I'm fighting everything in myself to not give up.

Almost the end of the hall.

One door left.

The final door is creaking open, and the heaviness of divinity fills the room. My inner wisdom blares. Somehow, I just know. It's my half. My intuition is screaming at me. My fingers are pins and needles. My whole body is numb. The noise in my head is silent.

This is it. I finally found you. I'm about to meet the love of my life, the reason I'm so fucked up, the reason I haven't been whole before. The room is dark. I hear footsteps.

The other half of my soul is walking towards me. My perfect fit, made for only me. You're a specimen of the gods, stolen from me by that sick rapist Zeus all those lifetimes ago. Everything feels dream-like. I'm so nervous I might throw up.

The lights aren't coming all the way on for some reason which is annoying, but I can see your form. I feel like I'm floating. I think I'm about to start crying. Or laughing. Or both. Actually, I think I'm going to pass out. What the hell is the matter with me? My hands are shaking and my teeth are almost chattering. I can't believe this is really happening. I always knew. I just had to have faith, that I had a reason to fight, that halves do find each other, that our destiny is better than I could ever imagine. That real love exists. Even for someone like me.

I can feel the needle piercing into my flesh, and I'm being pulled. A force like invisible strings or angel's wings or a hand of a god is moving us closer. If I reach out, I could almost touch you.

Then there's a static sound.

Something's wrong. My vision is fuzzy, even through my teary-eyed blur. Everything goes black except for the message appearing across the screen of my lenses:

GAME OVER

ERROR #9001zx-cc-a76/p: Transaction Failure.

We were unable to process your payment.

Please insert more e-coins to restart.

ABOUT THE AUTHOR

 **BELICIA RHEA WRITES** horror, weird fiction, and poetry. Her short fiction has been recognized in *Library Journal* and selected as a semifinalist for the 2023 Kurt Vonnegut Speculative Fiction Prize. She is the author of *Voracious*, her debut novella published by Dark Matter INK.

Also Available or Coming Soon from Dark Matter INK

Human Monsters: A Horror Anthology
Edited by Sadie Hartmann & Ashley Saywers
ISBN 978-1-958598-00-9

Zero Dark Thirty: The 30 Darkest Stories from Dark Matter Magazine, 2021–'22 Edited by Rob Carroll
ISBN 978-1-958598-16-0

Linghun by Ai Jiang
ISBN 978-1-958598-02-3

Monstrous Futures: A Sci-Fi Horror Anthology
Edited by Alex Woodroe
ISBN 978-1-958598-07-8

Our Love Will Devour Us by R. L. Meza
ISBN 978-1-958598-17-7

Haunted Reels: Stories from the Minds of Professional Filmmakers Curated by David Lawson
ISBN 978-1-958598-13-9

The Vein by Steph Nelson
ISBN 978-1-958598-15-3

Other Minds by Eliane Boey
ISBN 978-1-958598-19-1

Monster Lairs: A Dark Fantasy Horror Anthology
Edited by Anna Madden
ISBN 978-1-958598-08-5

Frost Bite by Angela Sylvaine
ISBN 978-1-958598-03-0

Free Burn by Drew Huff
ISBN 978-1-958598-26-9

The House at the End of Lacelean Street
by Catherine McCarthy
ISBN 978-1-958598-23-8

When the Gods Are Away by Robert E. Harpold
ISBN 978-1-958598-47-4

The Dead Spot: Stories of Lost Girls
by Angela Sylvaine
ISBN 978-1-958598-27-6

The Bleed by Stephen S. Schreffler
ISBN 978-1-958598-11-5

Grim Root by Bonnie Jo Stufflebeam
ISBN 978-1-958598-36-8

Beautiful Ways We Break Each Other Open
by Angela Liu
ISBN 978-1-958598-60-3

Abducted by Patrick Barb
ISBN 978-1-958598-37-5

Little Red Flags: Stories of Cults, Cons, and Control
Edited by Noelle W. Ihli & Steph Nelson
ISBN 978-1-958598-54-2

Frost Bite 2 by Angela Sylvaine
ISBN 978-1-958598-55-9

Dark Matter Presents: Fear City
ISBN 978-1-958598-90-0

Part of the Dark Hart Collection

Rootwork by Tracy Cross
ISBN 978-1-958598-01-6

Mosaic by Catherine McCarthy
ISBN 978-1-958598-06-1

Apparitions by Adam Pottle
ISBN 978-1-958598-18-4

I Can See Your Lies by Izzy Lee
ISBN 978-1-958598-28-3

A Gathering of Weapons by Tracy Cross
ISBN 978-1-958598-38-2

www.ingramcontent.com/pod-product-compliance
Lightning Source LLC
Chambersburg PA
CBHW021711190726
48289CB00008B/2483